Reverse Fairytales

Little Mermaid book 1

J.A.Armitage

Contents

The Erica Rose

"May God bless her and all who sail on her."

I cleared my throat, hoping I'd said it correctly, and gripped the bottle of champagne, terrified of letting it go too early or, worse still, missing the ship entirely.

Beyond the ship, the ocean shimmered in the midday sun. Diamond-like sparkles of light bounced off the calm cerulean water—water that looked so inviting, I wanted nothing more than to jump in, to surrender to the balmy ripples. Of course, wanting it and doing it were two different things. First of all, I couldn't swim, and secondly, my mother would pitch a fit if I took another step closer to the dock edge. She was already a bag of nerves from today's event.

I looked behind me, needing reassurance from my parents. This was my first official royal engagement, and I was terrified of messing it

4

up. My father beamed at me with pride while my mother gave me a thin smile. I could see the fear in her eyes although she was doing her best to hide it. I was amazed she'd come at all. The ocean positively terrified her. My father's hand was almost white with how hard my mother was squeezing it. Next to them, my little brother, Anthony, was picking his nose and examining the treasure he found up there. Not for the first time I was reminded how fortunate it was that I was the first in line to the throne.

Beside me, my life-long best friend nudged me to let go of the bottle. Officially, his title was Sir Hayden Harrington-Blythe, but to me, he was just Hayden. He'd been my first crush since our first day in kindergarten when he'd pulled on my pigtails, and I'd stamped on his foot. Despite our unpromising start, over the years we'd turned into friends. My crush on him was long since over, and his pigtail pulling days were long gone, but somehow, our friendship had survived.

"You do know you are supposed to let go of the bottle right?" whispered Hayden in my ear. I gave him a look I only ever reserved for him and lifted the bottle. Letting go, I watched it swing on a length of string, arcing towards the majestic ship's wooden hull. It made a tinkling sound as it smashed against the side of the ship, scattering glass all over the paved dock. I couldn't help thinking it was a waste of good champagne and that it would be better served at the ball being held in honor of my birthday in a couple of days' time. Still, I felt invigorated by the salty smell of the ocean, the atmosphere of a thousand happy people coming out to see the launch, and the fact that I now had a boat that bore my name. I was feeling as excited as I could hope to feel, second only to being allowed to actually go out on the damn thing.

The *Erica Rose's* white sails flapped in the breeze below the official flag of Trifork as if she were eager to be off, out onto the ocean. I couldn't blame her. To sail on the ocean was a lifelong dream of mine. Ever since I could remember, I'd looked out of my bedroom window toward the ocean and dreamed of the day that I'd be able to disappear beyond the rolling waves toward the horizon.

It was a dream that had never, and would never, be realized as long as my parents were in charge. For a kingdom so well-known for its naval and merchant vessels, my parents were ridiculously strict about letting me go near the ocean. This was the closest I'd gotten in the whole eighteen years of my life, and I had a full team of palace guards surrounding me, stopping me from taking one step closer to the water's edge than I had to. It was all because of my mother, of course. My father might have been the one that ruled Trifork, but in the palace, my mother was the one that wore the pants, so to speak. If my mother said I couldn't go near the ocean, then my father wasn't going to argue with her. However, today was a special day, and not even my mother could come up with a good enough reason for us not to be here. She might have been absolutely petrified, but she was the queen, a duty she held above everything, even crippling panic.

Everybody clapped as the wooden ship began pulling up its anchor, its crew readying themselves to set sail.

I took a deep breath and inhaled the salty air. Above the excited chatter of the crowd, seagulls cawed to each other as they flew overhead looking for an easy snack. Oh, how I envied them and their freedom.

My father managed to extricate himself from my mother's vice-like grip and joined me on the dock's edge. My poor mother's face turned even more ashen, and she had to grip a nearby railing instead to save herself from fainting. It was almost cruel, living so close to the ocean and being so frightened of it. I saw her eyes darting past my father and me to the ocean behind us as though it could somehow climb above the dock and swallow us whole. I don't doubt it could on a stormy day, but today the skies were blue, and the sea was calm.

"We here in Trifork have a rich sailing heritage, one of which I am immensely proud," began my father into the microphone that had been set up for the occasion. "Today is a big day for me, both as a king and a father. As you all know, my daughter, the princess Erica Rose, will turn eighteen in just two days' time. Her first official engagement was supposed to be at the ball, but she begged me to be allowed to launch this ship. Being the dutiful father I am, I agreed." He paused at this point waiting for a laugh. When he got it, he carried on. "This is my birthday gift to you, dear Erica. I know you've always had a fondness for the sea and so this ship not only bears your name but also belongs to you."

I blinked a couple of times, unsure if what I was hearing was true. The ship was mine? I wasn't allowed to dip my toes in the shallow waves at the beach, but I was allowed to own a ship?

I gazed up at the huge galleon. "She's mine?" Hope rose in my chest that I might, for the first time in my life, be able to go out on the ocean. My parents had never so much as let me sail in a dinghy before now, let alone go on a ship.

"She's all yours, sweetheart. As part of our fleet and a working ship, she will be taken out by her captain, Captain Jackson. But when she's back in Trifork, you will be able to see her whenever you want."

"See her?"

"Yes," beamed my father, oblivious to the disappointment I was feeling. Only see her? I didn't want a ship to look at. I'd spent my entire life watching the ships of Trifork sail in and out of the harbor. I wanted to sail to foreign lands, to feel the sea breeze upon my cheek. I wanted to know what it felt like to roll over the gentle waves with the vastness of the ocean the only thing in view.

My mother caught my disappointment though. She could read me like a book. An elegant woman with a sharp tongue and an even sharper sense of style, she swallowed her terror and took a few steps toward me, toward the ocean. She walked tall and calmly, but a slight tremor in her step gave her away.

"Aren't you happy with your new ship?"

"Yes ma'am," I lied. What was the point of having a ship if I wasn't allowed on it?

She flicked her eyes past me, once again, toward the ocean. What was it she was looking for? Her eyes snapped back to me. "You know my feelings on you going near the sea, Erica. It's a dangerous place. I nearly drowned when I was about your age." She took my hand and pulled me a couple of steps toward her—away from the dock's edge.

I'd heard the story a million times. Every time I even hinted at wanting to go near the sea, she'd dredge up the same story about how she nearly drowned when she was younger. I wasn't in the mood to hear it again.

The ship was cast off, the gangplank raised. My ship was about to go on an adventure I could only dream of. The wind caught the sails and the majestic vessel began to move, her crew waving at us as she inched away from the dockside.

My father clapped me on the back, a beaming smile on his face. Even my mother, who usually had a face like a prune when it came to anything to do with water, had found her smile again. I glanced over at Hayden. He knew I was disappointed. I talked about nothing but the ocean with him. He loved the water as I did, but unlike me, he could go out onto it whenever he wanted. He even had his own boat. It was nowhere near as grand as the *Erica Rose*, but at least, he was allowed to sail in it.

He flicked his eyes almost imperceptibly towards the ship. I arched a brow.

"Do it," he mouthed silently and cast his eyes towards the ship once again.

He wanted me to jump on the ship! He was actually daring me to do it. Thoughts of all the silly childhood pranks and adventures he'd led me into filled my mind. Hayden was the epitome of an irresistible bad idea. I followed his eye line to where the gangplank had been pulled up. The gate was still open, but it wouldn't be for long. The ship was already a foot away from the dock and moving swiftly towards the open sea. I had seconds to make a decision.

My heart hammered, and adrenaline took over. Without thinking too hard, I ran from my parents, barged past the palace guards, and jumped as far as I could right off the dock. The ship had moved much faster than I'd anticipated, and I missed the gate by a long shot, and instead of landing on the ship, I plunged head first into the sea.

All I could hear were my mother's screams as the water crowded in around me.

The water that had looked so warm and inviting when I'd been standing on the dock was actually a lot colder than I'd imagined, and as I scrambled for air, its icy grip took my breath away

Mouthfuls of briny water flowed into my mouth, causing me to choke as I tried desperately to keep above the water's surface.

In one terrifying instant, I realized what it was that my mother had been keeping me from for all these years. As I'd never been allowed in water deeper than a bath, I'd never learned how to swim. It occurred to me now that this wasn't exactly my finest moment.

The dress I'd had picked out for me, a knee length cotton blue dress was perfect for looking smart and launching a ship. It was utterly useless as a floatation device. The heavy, waterlogged fabric weighed me down, making it even harder to try to keep my head above water.

Beside me, I heard a splash. I looked over to see a red and white life ring bobbing close by with a rope attached to it. On the other end of the rope, the *Erica Rose's* crew shouted at me to grab hold. After I'd managed to pull myself through it, they heaved me up and pulled me over the side of the boat.

A group of worried faces peered down at me. One of the men reached a hand down to help me up. As I righted myself, my dress dripped ocean water all over the deck and tightened around me. I felt so uncomfortable in the soggy outfit, but when I saw how far from the dock we'd already moved, excitement flooded through me. The fear I'd felt just moments before dissolved, leaving me feeling exhilarated.

I was on a ship for the first time in my life, and we were sailing away from the dock.

With giddy excitement, I gripped a railing. On the edge of the dock, my parents shouted and waved for us to come back. My heart fell as I caught the expression on my mother's face. Her usual stern expression had contorted to one of absolute fear, and she wasn't trying to hide it anymore. Her screams pierced the air, her usual stoic facade dropped completely as she tore at my father who was desperately trying to pull her back from the edge of the dock.

Her fear of falling into the ocean was obviously smaller than losing one of her children to it.

My stomach churned as I realized the severity of my actions. I'd only wanted to go out to sea. I didn't want to hurt my mother in the process. I was going to be in the worst kind of trouble for this little stunt, and as we floated further and further out to sea, the more I realized that the adventure was not worth it.

Captain Jackson, a tall man with a perfectly groomed black mustache and oiled down hair greeted me with a salute. I'd never been saluted before. Bowed to and curtseyed aplenty, but a salute was new to me. I raised my hand and saluted back, unsure of the etiquette.

"I'm going to try to turn the ship back, your highness, but it may take a little time to adjust the sails. The wind is not optimal right now. There's a squall coming, and I'd hoped to get far enough away to miss it."

I glanced out to the horizon. The seamless blue sky was darkening, and the sea below it matched its threatening color. Where had that come from? Only seconds before, the weather had been as perfect as anyone could wish for.

"Yes, please turn around." My heart dropped as I realized that my adventure was over before it had even started, and I'd gotten nothing out of it except to embarrass myself in front of thousands of onlookers and terrify my poor mother.

I looked back over to the shoreline. My parents and all the onlookers were barely dots on the horizon now. To my right, I could see the public beach to which people flocked in the summer months. Beyond that were magnificent white cliffs that I'd heard plenty about but never actually seen before as they were only visible from the sea. To my left, the coast was much rockier, and here was where the royal castle stood. Only a wide promenade separated the rocks from the castle. It looked so dark and imposing with its granite grey towers; I barely recognized it from this angle.

"Why don't you go to my cabin and get changed out of those wet clothes. I'll have one of my crew show you where it is."

Captain Jackson swiveled on his toe and left me alone, feeling terrible. I'd not paused to consider the crew or the captain, and now they were going to have to abort their mission. I could chalk up a few more people to the list of those I'd disappointed. With a sigh, I walked to the other side of the deck to look out at the vast ocean. In the distance, the sea turned black and churned ominously almost as though that part of the ocean was alive and out to get us. It was a stark contrast to the crystal clear and calm water beneath the ship. Above me, the crew of the *Erica Rose* battled to maneuver the sails to turn us around.

"Your Royal Highness."

I heard someone shouting at me above the wind that was now blustering fiercely. Lightning forked, splitting the sky in two, and the wind tugged my hair from the clip that had been keeping it in place. Strands of long red hair whipped around my face. I turned to see a young man heading toward me.

"I'm Joe, Your Highness, the second in command of the *Erica Rose*," he said, giving me a quick bow. "The captain has asked me to escort you to his cabin."

Joe was barely older than me, with short, dirty blond hair and a winning smile. I was surprised to see someone so young be the second in command of such a ship.

"It's getting a little choppy," Joe cautioned, his cheeks red as he took my hand. "They are going to struggle to get the ship back to shore. The forecast mentioned a little bit of turbulent water, but it looks to be shaping up to be a proper storm out there."

I followed Joe to a big wooden doorway, which he opened for me and beckoned me inside. As I thanked him, a boom filled the darkening sky.

"Thunder," Joe remarked, taking my hand and leading me down a corridor. I held on tightly to him as the ship listed violently to one side from the sharp turn of the wheel. He showed me to a large room with a writing desk on one side and a bed on the other.

"There will be some clothes in the wardrobe there," he said, pointing to a small door. "I don't expect the captain has any dresses, but I'm sure you'll find something dry to wear."

I watched the storm unfold through a small porthole as Joe left me to help the captain. It seemed no one was expecting the weather to be this bad and how could they? Only ten minutes earlier, there hadn't been a cloud in the sky, and now there was barely any blue left, only the darkness of the sea and the sky. It was strange how quickly the storm had taken hold. I certainly had never seen anything like it before. Outside, the rain began to lash down, pitter-pattering on the round window. Thunder crashed as the waves became more intense with the roaring wind that whipped all around us. The storm had sneaked up on us quickly, and as far as I could see, we were getting further and further away from the coastline. Whatever Captain Jackson's men were doing to turn the ship around, it wasn't helping.

I hated admitting it to myself after dreaming of the day I could finally sail on the sea for so long, but I was beginning to get scared. My mother's screams echoed in my head, although we had drifted too far to really hear her. The boat creaked with the strain, and from out of the window, I could see we were being pulled closer and closer toward the storm. A crash from behind me made me jump. I turned to find that some previously neatly stacked dishes had been flung from the cupboard and were now in hundreds of pieces on the floor. Holding on was almost impossible, the ship was lurching so much. I tried walking over to the wardrobe that Joe had pointed out, but the floor beneath me was rocking so much under the motion of the waves that I could barely stand at all. With a shock, I saw a stream of water pushing the remnants of the dishes across the floor. It was coming from the doorway. We were taking on water. I held on to the writing desk to keep myself upright, but the motion of the ship knocked me to the floor. Something sharp pierced my side, and when I looked down, I saw a sliver of broken plate had cut through my dress and into my flesh creating a bloom of fresh blood on the wet fabric.

I looked up to grab hold of the desk to pull myself back up and was shocked to see that the window was now partly submerged. We were sinking, and we were sinking fast. Pulling myself up, I ran to the door quickly. I had to get out, or I would drown. I yanked the door as hard as I could, and as it opened, a deluge of water rushed in knocking me over once again. The lights flickered out leaving me in complete darkness as the water engulfed me, sending me flying into something hard. Water filled my lungs as the blackness folded in around me, my mother's warnings of the fierceness of the ocean echoing in my head.

Saved

Soft lips touched mine and softly blew into my mouth.

What was happening? Was I being kissed? Why?

I coughed roughly, and salt water flooded into my mouth, except it was coming up rather than going in. Someone rolled me forcefully onto my side, and the salty water trickled out.

I coughed again and opened my eyes. One minute I was being kissed, the next my lungs were screaming in agony, and I was coughing up half the ocean. Sunlight flooded my retinas as I opened my eyes, causing me to blink a few times. Sunlight? Hadn't it been dark just a moment ago? I closed my eyes again, not ready for the brightness.

"Are you ok?" a voice asked. It was a man's voice. Probably the same man who had pushed me onto my side, the same man who had kissed me. His accent was very strange, and I couldn't place it, but his deep voice was warm and comforting. I'd not traveled much, but I'd met many visitors from other lands, and he sounded like none of them. He certainly wasn't from any of the nine kingdoms.

I nodded my head and promptly threw up. An acidic taste filled my mouth as the contents of my stomach, mostly salt water and a bit of breakfast, emptied out of me.

I wasn't alright, but I'd been schooled long enough not to show my feelings.

"You don't look it," the voice replied. The man attached to it gently moved my hair from my face, leaving me exposed to the sun. It beat down on my cheek warming it. I opened my eyes again, this time readying myself for the brightness. In front of me, was the most beautiful man I'd ever seen in my life. I couldn't call him handsome. The word handsome reminded me of men in suits. This man was striking with piercing green eyes and black hair so long, it was almost down to his waist. I'd never seen a man with long hair before. Everyone in my life had been presented to me perfectly turned out, wearing only the finest of clothing. This guy wasn't even wearing a shirt. His bare chest glistened with water dripping from his wet hair. As I gazed up at him, a flash of purple came over his eyes. A second later, they were green again. I blinked, mesmerized by what I'd seen or what I thought I'd seen.

"Princess!" I heard a voice shouting from far away. The man heard it too. He cocked his head up and to the side. Following his gaze, I saw some men at the top of the cliffs. I blinked a couple of more times and glanced at my surroundings. We were on a tiny beach inaccessible except by the water. I had been laid out on a flat rock by the water's edge, and my savior was half in and half out of the water. Perhaps, he'd come across me when he'd been out swimming? Beyond him, the sea had returned to a shimmering blue and the sky was once again cloudless. It was like the storm hadn't happened at all.

"They are looking for you," said the man, pulling me away from my thoughts. "I think you'll be ok now."

I looked back at him again, shocking myself at how deeply irresistible I found him. My head pounded, and my throat felt as though someone had used sandpaper roughly on it, and yet, all I could think of was the way his lips had felt upon mine.

"Kiss me again." Just saying it shocked me to my core. I didn't know where I was or how I got there, and here I was asking a perfect stranger to kiss me. I wondered if I'd suffered a concussion at some point. My head certainly hurt enough. And yet...I meant it. I wanted to feel the taste of his lips again. The last time, I'd been half asleep.

He gave me a confused grin. "Again?"

"Your Highness!" It was that voice again from the cliff above. I wished it would go away. The very edges of my consciousness were hazy, and my memory was blurred. It was like everything in my past was just out of reach. I knew I was the royal princess, heir to the throne of Trifork. I also knew I was at the base of one of Trifork's famous white cliffs. Beyond that, everything, including how I ended up on a beach with a half-naked man, was floating just beyond my grasp.

"I've got to go," said the man. "You'll be ok." He disappeared out of my line of sight. I tried sitting up to see where he went, but the effort made me feel dizzy again. I scanned the shoreline, but there was nobody there. Out in the distance, I thought I saw a ripple on the surface of the ocean, but darkness was closing in again. I closed my eyes and once again succumbed to unconsciousness.

I woke to find myself in the palace infirmary.

With over three hundred staff working and living in the palace, not to mention my accident-prone brother, my father had had the small hospital built in one of the palace wings a few years ago after a bad strain of flu had left half of the staff ill.

The infirmary was quite cheerful for a hospital. A rainbow of color decorated the painted white walls thanks to the light coming through a large circular stained-glass window depicting the founder of Trifork. A strong, floral scent invaded my senses, and a brief glance around showed me it was coming from a vase of lilies in the corner of the room.

Beside my bed, I found my mother. Without her usual perfect makeup she appeared pale, almost a ghost of her usual self. Dark circles had taken up residence under her eyes, eyes which were bloodshot from lack of sleep. Her hand held mine. It felt warm and reassuring, although her grip was a little too tight. I tried to sit up, but the effort made me feel sick.

"What happened?" I croaked. My throat burned with the effort of speaking. Goodness only knew just how much sea water I'd swallowed.

"Just lay back, honey," she replied, letting go of my hand and plumping my pillow. Honey? She never called me honey. She never called me anything but Erica. When she sat back down, I noticed she'd been crying.

My memory of earlier was slipping, as if an invisible hand had reached into my brain and started pulling at the fibers, spilling all my memories from the last day. Her tears reminded me of something, but I couldn't remember what. My mother never cried. I had a feeling that those tears were because of something I'd done, but I couldn't remember what. A fog had descended into my brain distorting everything.

My mother pressed her lips together and stared down at the bed as though she was weighing what to tell me. When she looked back up, I saw that the tears had returned. "You almost drowned. For a while, we thought you had drowned. The ship went down in a storm yesterday. We sent thousands of people out looking for you, but it was only this morning one of our volunteers found you. He brought you straight here."

This morning? I'd been out all night?

"He had long hair?" I asked, remembering my strange encounter on the beach. I felt my cheeks begin to redden as I recalled what I'd said to him. I'd asked him to kiss me. Oh, I hoped he'd not told my parents that. I'd never live it down.

"No honey. It was just one of the palace guards." She looked confused. "What makes you think he had long hair?"

"I saw him. He had long hair, and he disappeared." I tried to get a clear picture of him in my head through the fog but failed. Just like the events of the previous twenty-four hours, he was slipping from my mind.

My mother's brows knitted together, and she pursed her lips. Without saying anything, she brought her hand up to my forehead to feel for a fever.

"There was no one on that beach with you, sweetheart. You were completely alone when you were found, and there couldn't have been anyone down there with you because the beach you washed up on was cut off from all sides. We had to get someone with a rope to scale the cliff to get down to you, and you were pulled up by the same rope on a stretcher."

I'd not dreamed it. He'd definitely been there. Surely, I couldn't have made him up. Everything about him was drifting from my mind, and yet, I could remember his distinctive voice so clearly. "He swam out to sea then?" I ventured.

She shook her head and took my hand again. "The sea is very dangerous at that part of the coast. I'm told that it was a fluke that you managed to swim to the beach without your body being bashed against the rocks."

I hadn't swum to the beach though, had I? I'd either floated there or been brought there. The question was, if I'd been brought there, who was it that brought me and where did he go if he wasn't on the beach when I was found?

"What about Joe and the captain?" I asked realizing I wouldn't get anywhere trying to solve that particular mystery.

My mother's eyes began brimming with tears once again. "I'm so sorry, honey. The *Erica Rose* went down in the storm. We've still got people out there looking for the crew, but it's been over twenty hours since the storm, and you are the only person we've found."

My ship had gone down, and it looked like all her crew had gone down with her. I thought back to being onboard. A memory came to the surface. I snatched at it, thinking of all the details of the captain's quarters before it went back into the fuzz. I'd been trapped inside there. If anyone should have died on that ship, it was me. All the others were on deck when the storm hit. If I had managed to survive while unconscious, then they should have survived too.

"They are still out there," I insisted. It didn't make sense otherwise. "Don't stop the search."

She gave me a sad smile. "We'll keep the search going for a while, but it doesn't look good."

Lucy, the head nurse came into the infirmary. When she saw I was awake, she hurried over. Without speaking, she popped a thermometer into my mouth and took my wrist presumably to check my pulse.

I closed my eyes to block everything out.

My heart felt heavy at the loss of the crew members. I'd only met them yesterday, but it hurt to think of them dying on the maiden voyage of my ship. And yet, a part of me still couldn't accept that they were dead. We'd been pulled away from the shore by the storm, and yet, I'd ended up there. I'd somehow gotten to the beach without remembering it. Without even being conscious it seemed, and a mysterious stranger who looked like no one I'd ever seen before in my life kissed me before disappearing into thin air. None of it made sense. I wondered if my brain had made up the whole thing and if the man with the long hair had been a dream. My head pounded just thinking about it all.

I heard my mother chatting away to Lucy, oblivious to the turmoil going on inside me. She was asking if I'd be alright enough to attend the ball tomorrow.

Tomorrow! I'd somehow lost a day.

"I don't know," replied Lucy. "She's had a bump to the head and lost quite a bit of blood. I did my best to sew the wound in her side up, it was just a shallow flesh wound, but she is still very weak. It might be better to postpone it for a bit."

I opened my eyes and pulled out the thermometer with my free hand and gave it back to the nurse.

"I'm fine," I lied. Before Lucy had mentioned the cut in my side, I'd forgotten about it, but now I knew it was there. I could feel it. Lucy had tightly bandaged it, but below the bandage, I could feel the sharp pain of stitches. I wasn't about to tell my mother that, though. She'd been through enough in the last couple of days thanks to me and my idiocy. "I want to go."

My mother had been planning this party for months. I'd seen how much effort and planning had gone into it. It wasn't as simple as postponing it. Everything was ready. The grand hall had been decorated for the better part of a week. The caterers had already started preparing the food, and over a thousand dignitaries from the nine kingdoms had been invited. Postponing it would be a nightmare of epic proportions.

My mother looked at me with nothing but concern in her eyes. "Are you sure? You don't have to if you aren't well enough. I can ask your father to put it back a couple of months."

Even as she said it, I could see that she didn't want to put it off. The way she was being so sweet to me now wasn't like her. The shock of nearly losing her daughter to the thing she feared most had changed her. It was then I remembered my mother's screams after I fell into the water. Ear piercing screams of pure terror. I'd done that to her. I'd caused that fear. A lump came to my throat as I looked into her eyes, eyes the blue-green color of the ocean she hated so much.

I took her hands in mine and smiled. "I wouldn't miss it for the world."

She jumped up and clapped her hands together. "I'll tell Alexander not to call anyone. He'll be so pleased. I think I've been driving him mad with all the talk of this ball. He'll be down to see you shortly."

I suppressed a smile. My mother had run the whole gamut of emotion in the last day or so. I'd never seen her like this before. She was usually so rigid and composed. Now she was as giddy as a school girl.

"If she's going to the ball, she needs her rest," Lucy asserted, ushering my mother away from my bed. "Her father will have to wait."

My mother's eyes flashed with excitement. "I should go and let the dressmaker know that you will be needing your gown after all," she trilled. I'd never seen her so excited. I waited until she left the room completely and closed my eyes pretending to be asleep. I didn't want the nurse poking me or prodding me anymore. I just wanted to be left alone with my thoughts.

As soon as I closed my eyes, there he was. I could see him again—the man with the long hair. I was sure I'd not made him up. How could I have? In my mind's eye, I could see him so clearly. His chiseled chin and straight nose, his muscular chest and those eyes, those stunning green eyes that flashed purple.

He was so unusual and yet so real; but at the same time, he was impossible. My mother had said it herself. No one could survive swimming through those rocks to get to the shore, and yet, I had. I'd survived and somehow done it while being unconscious. The whole thing was beyond belief. I hadn't just washed up on that beach. Someone had to have brought me there.

My mind was still whirling when Lucy came to me with some hot chocolate. The delicious smell of it had me opening my eyes.

"I wasn't sure if you were sleeping or just resting your eyes," she remarked, placing the chocolate beside my bed along with a couple of pills. "These will really make you sleep and help with the pain. You want to be fresh for your big day tomorrow. Oh, and these are for you."

She handed me a hand-picked bunch of daisies.

"Hayden's been here?" I asked. As a princess, I was often given flowers. Huge expensive bouquets wrapped with ribbon. As a young child, I'd remarked how much I preferred wild daisies and the next day at school, he'd shown up with a bunch that he'd picked from a nearby field. Since then, on my birthday every year, he'd brought me daisies.

She placed the daisies on the bedside cabinet, not bothering to find a vase for them. "He came while you were sleeping. I told him you weren't well enough to see anyone today. He said to tell you he'd see you tomorrow at the ball."

I smiled, picturing his face, his dark blond hair never falling quite as it should, usually falling over one of his deep brown eyes, and the cheeky grin that almost permanently resided on his face. In my mind, the picture shifted. The brown eyes became green, the hair darkened, and the grin turned into full, smiling

31

lips. What was it with the stranger? I couldn't seem to get him out of my mind.

"Lucy? Do you think what happened to me could make me see things that aren't real?"

"Like hallucinations?" she asked, looking all worried again.

"No, more like fake memories."

She put her hand on my forehead again, no doubt checking to see if I had a fever. "You did have a bump to the head. Sometimes your brain tries to make sense of things, which can cause dreams to seem real. The best thing you can do is sleep and see how you feel in the morning."

She turned the lights down low as she left. I picked up the pills and chased them down with the hot chocolate. She was right about one thing, I really needed to sleep. I closed my eyes and let oblivion wash over me.

The Stranger

"How are you feeling?" My mother asked the second I opened my eyes. I noticed she was already in full makeup as she passed me a mug of coffee and two painkillers.

I drank the whole thing down, using it as an excuse to decide how to answer her question. On the one hand, I felt pretty good, considering. My headache was gone, and I no longer felt dizzy or sick. Whatever had been in those pills that Lucy had given me had done the trick, and I'd slept well. On the other hand, my heart still felt heavy over the loss of my ship's crew. I'd not known them, but it didn't stop me feeling terrible about what happened. I could also still see the stranger clearly in my mind. The pills hadn't taken that away.

I went with "I'm fine," because it was what she wanted to hear.

"Wonderful," she clapped her hands together as she always did when she was excited about something. "I'll see if Lucy will release you, and then we'll get you ready for the ball."

Twenty minutes later, I found myself in my mother's dressing room with her bevy of beauticians. One started on my hair, teasing my long red locks into something manageable.

"Up or down, Your Highness?" I knew the question was directed at my mother, and so, I waited for her to answer. I'd never been allowed to decide what to wear or how to have my hair on occasions like these. My mother always had the final say.

She came up to me and looked at my reflection. Once upon a time, she had the same vibrant red hair as I did, but now, hers had dimmed with age and had more gray than red. Other than that, we looked remarkably similar. We had the same heart-shaped face and long eyelashes. My lips and green eye color I'd inherited from my father. Just thinking of green eyes reminded me of the stranger again. What was it about him that kept popping up in my brain? Was it the fact that it looked like I'd somehow made him up, my brain rearranging normality into something else? My eyes were a perfectly normal shade of green with flecks of brown in them. The stranger's eyes. They were the brightest green eyes I'd ever seen, almost otherworldly and the only flecks they had in them were flecks of light just like the light I'd seen bouncing off the waves when I'd first boarded the *Erica Rose.* And then, there was that purple flash. Now that couldn't be real. No one's eyes changed color like that. It just wasn't possible. I had to give in to the fact that Lucy was probably right, and my brain had simply conjured him up out of nowhere.

"Erica, are you alright?" My mother gazed at me in concern.

"I'm sorry, mother. I was just daydreaming. What did you say?"

"I said, it's up to you how you have your hair. Do you want it up or down?"

I hadn't yet seen what my dress looked like, but I knew it would be a deep purple color. On anyone else, the purple would have looked magnificent, but with my red hair, it was sure to clash. Purple was the traditional color of our royal family, and so for generations, Royal princes and princesses had been wearing it for occasions such as these. Unfortunately, when my great-great-great grandparents started this tradition, they didn't foresee a time when one of their descendants would have flaming red hair that would look ridiculous with purple. My own mother had taken to wearing lilac these days just to tone things down.

I sighed and looked at myself in the mirror. My hair reached almost down to my waist, cascading down in loose waves. It would have been nice to wear it down, to show it off, but in the end, I decided it would be far better to minimize it and have it put up.

The hairdresser nodded his head and got to work while the young woman who was doing my makeup, dithered between the colors on her palette.

"Just make it neutral," I suggested. "Nothing goes with red and purple, so I'm screwed whatever you do."

"Erica! Language!" my mother admonished, but the young makeup artist gave me a grin and began to mix some pale beiges together to use as foundation.

The end result was much better than I'd expected. The hairdresser had put a tiara on my up-do which hid most of the red, and the makeup artist had done an excellent job not making me look too garish.

Once we were finished, my mother sent everyone away, so it was just she and I. She took me into her bedroom and sat me on the bed.

"You look stunning today. I have never been so proud in my life to have a daughter as wonderful as you. You've grown up into such a beautiful young lady; it will be a pleasure to show you off tonight."

Tonight was not only my birthday party but a coming out party where I was to be formally introduced to the people of Trifork.

"Have you been practicing your speech?" she asked.

A few weeks earlier, I'd been asked to prepare a speech, which with a little help, I'd done. I'd read it so often, I knew the whole thing by heart. I nodded my head and fished around for the piece of paper I'd written it on.

"I feel so nervous."

She put her arm around me and drew me into a hug. "It's to be expected. I was terrified the day your grandparents threw an engagement party for your father and me. I was expected to give a speech then too."

"How was it?"

She shrugged. "I can't remember. I'd drunk quite a lot of champagne."

Her admission shocked me. I'd never seen my mother drunk. It was weird to think of her that way. She laughed at me and gave me a wink. "Don't worry. No one could tell."

The happy look on her face dissolved into one of sadness.

"I'm sorry about your ship sinking. I know you've found these past couple of days difficult. We all have, but your father and I have got another surprise for you. I hope it makes up for it."

I sat up straight "What is it?"

She stood up and walked towards the door. "You'll see," she answered cryptically. "I'll send someone up to get you when the ball starts. Your dress is hung up in the closet. I hope you like it." And with that, she was gone.

I rose slowly, not sure what to expect. I'd given my mother instructions on how I wanted my dress to look. I'd asked for nothing too fancy, but my mother had a tendency to go overboard with these kinds of things.

I opened the door to find a long, silk, sleeveless dress with a band around the waist. It was only when I took it out into the light of my mother's chandelier that I saw how magnificent it really was. It was iridescent, shining first purple then green depending on the light – almost like magic. The stranger's eyes once again flashed through my mind. Something about the dress reminded me of him. I shook the thought off and pulled the dress over my head, being careful not to ruin my hair or makeup. In the mirror, stood a princess. While the purple clashed with my hair, the green complimented it. My mother had picked this strange material on purpose so

I could look beautiful while still keeping to tradition.

I gave myself a twirl. The light reflected off my skirt as it flew out all around me, giving the impression of a stormy sea. I looked striking. In all the years of wearing pretty dresses, I'd never seen myself in something so gorgeous, something that made me beautiful. I almost couldn't tear my eyes away from my reflection.

I had to practice my speech though, so I spent the next hour going through it in my head. I wanted to sound confident, but now that it was so close, I was positive that the whole thing sounded ridiculous—like the ramblings of a three-year-old who didn't know what she was talking about.

When the knock on the door sounded, I almost had a heart attack. Fear gripped me as I realized that this was it. There was no more time to prepare. I was to be taken down to the great hall by one of the palace staff, and there I had to walk out and greet every one of the six hundred people who were there to see me.

I took a deep breath as I opened the door. In front of me, stood Hayden with a bouquet of flowers. A big bouquet of stargazer lilies and twenty other types of flowers I didn't know the name of. They must have cost him a fortune.

"Where are my daisies?" I teased as I let him in. From behind his back, he pulled out a bunch of daisies tied together with an old bit of string.

"Someone asked me to bring these up to you," he said, placing the bouquet down on a nearby table, "and these are from me." He handed me the daisies. As the son of Lord Harrington-Blythe, he had more money than he could spend in a lifetime. He could have afforded a hundred bouquets of flowers, but oh, how I loved those daisies. I ran to the bathroom and filled a glass with water, placing the daisies in it before setting them down on the table.

"Don't you need water for the big bunch?" he asked pointing at the expensive bouquet.

"I'll get a maid to bring a vase up," I replied, kissing his cheek. I'd never been so pleased to see him as I was now. If anyone could keep me from dying of stage fright, it was Hayden. I took his hand, and together, we headed down to the great hall.

"How are you feeling?" Hayden asked as we stood behind the large golden doors that led into the great hall. All the guests would be lined up waiting to shake my hand—all six hundred of them. It made me feel sick just thinking about it. "Your mother told me that you've been having a tough time. She said you'd been hallucinating."

"I've been better," I admitted. My headache was now more of a dull pain, thanks to the painkillers, but my side hurt, and I still felt a little foggy. "My mother is wrong. Someone, a man, saved my life. He brought me to the beach where I was found and gave me CPR."

Hayden looked at me curiously. "You hallucinated a man?" His eyes gleamed as if this was somehow funny.

"I didn't hallucinate anything. The man was real."

Why did no one believe me?

"Ok. If you say he is real, then I believe you."

I could tell he was lying to appease me. He kissed my cheek and turned to leave.

"Where are you going?" I asked him in a panic. I didn't want to go in there alone.

He pointed down the corridor that ran the entire length of the ballroom. "I have to go in through the catering entrance so I can join the line to formally greet you. I'll see you soon, don't worry."

"I can't do this!" I cried, desperately trying to keep my breathing even.

He kissed me on the cheek again, calming my nerves. "This is your big night. You have to go in there alone. I'll be with you once you finish formally meeting everyone. Maybe after you've shaken hands with all the old fogies, we can play hooky and steal some food from the kitchens."

"We are being served a seven-course meal," I replied to which he grinned. He gave me a wave as he jogged down the corridor.

I took a deep breath and nodded my head at the guards at the door. They slowly pulled them open, and as they did, I heard the sound of clapping. The long line of people waiting to greet me stretched right around the hall. Thankfully, I only had to spend a couple of seconds with each person, or I'd have been greeting people for the rest of the night. To my right, stood my mother, father, and Anthony, who would follow me down the line and greet everyone in turn. To my left, the line began. A member of the staff had a list and began to read out the names as I shook hands in turn. The first people to greet me were Hayden's parents. I'd known them all my life. They were my parent's best friends and very high-up members of society. Lord Harrington-Blythe was the Admiral for the Navy of Trifork, while his wife spoke for many charities and organized fundraisers.

I gave them both a warm smile as the page read out their names. Lord Harrington-Blythe, or Henry as I knew him, took my hand and kissed it warmly, before giving me a grin through his bushy gray mustache. Lady Harrington-Blythe, or Evaine, to her friends, politely shook my hand, although I could tell she really wanted to bring me in for a hug.

I walked down the line, nodding, smiling, and shaking hands as I had been taught to do. I thanked every single person for coming and tried in vain to remember all their names. About two-thirds of the way down the line, just after I'd greeted Queen Charmaine and her husband, Prince Cynder of Silverwood, the page faltered. He'd been just about to read out a name when he stumbled and pulled the paper up to look at the continuing list below. I gave him a sharp look, raising my eyebrows. He just shrugged his shoulders. I turned back to the line, ready to see whom he'd got lost on. With any luck, I'd know them and could help the page find his place. It was then that I realized why he'd stopped. Right in front of me was the stranger—the figment of my imagination, the product of my bump on the head. He was real, and he was standing there as clear as day, a smile on his face and a look of amusement in his eyes.

To top it off, he was even more gorgeous than I remembered.

A dance and a kiss

I waited for him to speak, to say his name, anything; but he remained silent. Instead, he took my hand and brought it up to his lips. The way he looked at me as he did, never taking his eyes off me, eyes that reminded me so much of the dress I was wearing hypnotized me. They were one color one minute, another color the next. I was in dire danger of getting completely lost in them.

My heart must have been beating a mile a minute because I lost all composure along with my mind. The words I'd been trained to say, the same words I'd literally just repeated four hundred times had flown completely out of my mind, leaving me speechless.

"Thank you for coming," I managed to finally get out through the fog in my head. In the back of my mind, I was aware that all eyes were on me, wondering what was happening. I wasn't even sure what was happening myself, but it was becoming obvious that I'd already spent more than my allotted ten seconds with him. He nodded his response. His eyes crinkled up at the edges as his lips widened into a smile, exposing dimples in his cheeks. Just that small gesture made my heart nearly fly out of my chest.

I knew I'd waited too long. People were beginning to notice that I'd turned to mush, and I was sure it was pretty obvious that the pink of my cheeks now clashed with my hair *and* my dress. Thankfully, the page saved me by calling out the name of the person next to him. Princess Carabosse of Eshen. I gave her a quick smile while internally trying not to fall apart. I probably would have too if my parents hadn't been in the receiving line right behind me. I could only imagine their confusion at the stranger, but as many of the people we'd invited were dignitaries and royalty from other kingdoms, I doubted they knew many of the people here anyway. They'd probably pass him off as a prince from a far-off land. Maybe he was. He was certainly foreign-looking. No one I'd ever met had eyes quite the same color as his, and absolutely no men in Trifork kept their hair long.

Greeting the rest of the people seemed to take forever. The never-ending line of people smiling and offering me congratulations, blurred from one person to the next. It took everything I had to keep to protocol and not gaze back up the line to where he was standing.

Finally, after getting a quick kiss on both cheeks from princess Ala from Ling, I reached Hayden who was the last in line. As we exchanged inane pleasantries, the orchestra in the corner began to play.

"Shall we?" he asked, taking my hand. It had been planned that Hayden would be my first dance, which is why he'd stationed himself at the end of the line. My mother had asked me who I wanted to dance with, and I'd not hesitated to ask for my life-long best friend. Now though, my thoughts were with the stranger. Where had he come from? How had he gotten in, and why hadn't he spoken?

Hayden led me to the center of the room, and the orchestra began to play a slow waltz. My mother had picked the music and organized dancing lessons, which I'd been taking for the past three months. Hayden bowed to me, and I curtseyed before he once again took my hand, and we began our heavily rehearsed dance routine.

I gazed around the room, but now that Hayden and I had started dancing, everyone else had joined in. The room was awash with beautiful swirling dresses of all colors. The stranger was nowhere to be seen.

"Are you ok? You seem a little distracted. Is it something to do with that strange man in the lineup?"

I felt my cheeks redden at Hayden's words. He looked at me so intently; it was almost as if he was trying to read my mind. If Hayden had noticed the stranger, it stood to reason that everyone else would have too.

"What strange man?" I asked, pretending that the stranger wasn't completely filling my thoughts. "Oh, the one where the page forgot his name. I don't know what happened there. No, I'm just thinking about how lucky I am that so many people came out for my ball."

I tried sounding as nonchalant as possible, hoping that Hayden wouldn't probe me further. Now that I knew the stranger was real and not just a figment of my imagination, I wanted to find out more about him, before telling anyone else. No one believed he existed anyway, and I decided then and there to keep it that way for now.

"Is it my amazing groovy dance moves that're putting you off then because you're missing out by looking in every direction but at me."

"What?" I asked, my eyes turning back to Hayden. "Oh yeah, erm, no, erm, sorry. What did you say?"

Hayden gave me his goofy grin and wiggled his eyebrows. "I said my groovy dance moves."

"Groovy?" I laughed. No one had used that term in like a billion years. "You have two left feet."

"Surely not?" he replied with mock sincerity.

"You know it, I know it, and my poor feet that you've stepped on three times certainly know it. Don't you remember anything from our dance lessons?"

A swish of gold passed near to us causing me to change the subject. "Astrid looks lovely this evening."

Hayden cast his eyes to the right where Astrid was dancing with her father. Astrid was one of the ladies of the court, a good friend of mine, and Hayden's girlfriend. I'd asked her a few weeks ago if she minded me having the first dance with Hayden, and of course, she hadn't. There wasn't a jealous bone in her body. Not that she had anything to be jealous of. She knew that I didn't have a boyfriend and was more than happy to let me borrow him for one dance so I wouldn't have to get up and do the traditional first dance alone.

"She does, doesn't she?" He smiled a soppy smile, the kind I'd only ever seen on him during the past few months of dating Astrid. Just seeing how smitten he was made me think of the stranger again. I still couldn't see him in the crowd of dancers.

"Did you see that guy?" I murmured, glancing about me once again.

Hayden raised an eyebrow and looked around as if he was searching for him. "What guy? The guy in the lineup? You do know him!"

"Yeah, sorry I lied. He's the guy who saved me from drowning the other day. He wasn't invited, he just kind of showed up, but I can't see him now."

Hayden adopted a look of concern and stopped dancing. "Do you want me to get security?"

"No, it's ok. He's probably already left."

Hayden shook his head. "He's probably here to ask for a reward now that he knows who you are. I'll bet you a dollar that you'll find him trying to extort money from your parents."

"A dollar?"

He slipped his hand into his pocket and brought out a silver dollar. "It's all I have on me."

I pushed it back into his pocket. "Keep it. I don't think he's like that. Besides I can see my parents talking to your mother at the far end of the hall."

"Can I cut in?" We both turned to see Astrid. She had such an expectant smile on her lovely face. She wore a yellow dress that went beautifully with her long, golden hair. She was simply breathtaking.

"Of course," I replied, taking a step back from Hayden. Now that everyone else was dancing, Hayden and I had fulfilled what was expected of us.

He still looked worried "Are you going to be ok?"

I nodded as the tune changed and dashed through the dancers to the edge of the great hall.

There were many people sitting in the seats around the edge of the hall, but he wasn't among them. Where was he? Surely, he'd not turned up just to shake my hand and then disappear? What would be the point of that?

I was beginning to wonder if I'd hallucinated him for a second time when I noticed the doors to the balcony were open. Outside, the sounds of the waves of the ocean were now audible over the sound of the music playing inside. Our castle was situated on a cliff overlooking the ocean, which is where I got my love of the water from. I'd often sit on my own balcony and just watch the waves breaking over the rocks below or watching the seabirds catching fish. I headed to the open doors, full of expectation. I couldn't help it. My heart was hammering in my chest at the thought he might be out there.

Tonight, the view was especially spectacular. The full moon shone brightly casting a thousand diamonds over the sea. I took a deep breath of salty air and looked around the balcony. It wasn't a real balcony, as such, since it extended right down to the lower level of the palace via a set of steps leading out to our private promenade. It was empty. I gazed over the edge expecting to be disappointed, but there he was. Just standing there looking out over the ocean, the moon lighting him from behind giving him a kind of angelic aura.

I held back, unsure of what to do. To go down the steps and leave my own party would be considered rude by my parents, but not to, oh, that would be a thousand times worse. Sneaking a peek over my shoulder to see that no one had spotted me leaving the great hall, I took my first steps outside. I passed a guard who looked at me questioningly despite being trained to keep his eyes forward. "I'm just getting some fresh air," I told him, though it was none of his business what I was doing outside.

Taking the first step was hard, but once I'd started, I knew there was no going back. It became easier with each step that I took.

The stranger had his back to me as I reached the bottom of the steps. His hair blew in the slight breeze.

"Hello," I ventured nervously. Excitement coursed through my veins, pushed by my hammering heart.

He turned and smiled at me causing my heart to almost stop. What was wrong with me? I was positively giddy which wasn't princess-like at all. I tried to rein it in, to appear nonchalant.

"I'm glad to see you here," I began, taking in those eyes of his. Even with the moonlight to the back of him, they still sparkled, almost like the ocean. "I want to thank you for saving me the other day."

He didn't move, didn't speak, just stood there looking at me, making me feel more self-conscious than I already was.

"I should apologize too," I flustered. "I shouldn't have asked you to kiss me. I realize now that you were doing CPR. I can't begin to tell you how embarrassed I felt when I woke up and rememb..."

I had to stop talking midway through the sentence. He'd walked right up to me; his face was mere inches from mine, and I'd quite forgotten what I was going to say, or how to talk at all.

Seconds later, it didn't matter. My lips were being put to better use than talking.

He leaned forward and kissed me lightly.

I couldn't breathe from the excitement coursing through me. If I'd have known leaving my own party would feel so good, I'd have skipped the first dance with Hayden altogether.

He tasted like the ocean. Somehow, it didn't surprise me. He was connected to it in some way; I just didn't know how.

I leaned right into him, turning a light peck on the lips to something so much more. I think I surprised him with the voracity with which I kissed him, but he matched my urgency before eventually pulling away. I might have been mistaken, but there was a slight blush to his cheeks. I hated to think what my cheeks looked like; I could feel them burning with both shock and excitement.

He glanced up toward the balcony from which I could still hear the faint strains of music over the sound of the ocean. He took my hand and wrapped his other arm around my waist. Slowly, he began to turn me. I realized he was dancing with me. It was so unlike dancing with Hayden and his "groovy" moves or with my dance teacher, Stephan, whom my mother had brought in specially from Silverwood to teach me how to dance.

No, we weren't dancing at all; we were moving on air. My feet barely touched the ground as he guided me effortlessly around. I'd never known it was possible to move the way he did, or the way I did with him. I closed my eyes and rested my head on his shoulder. He smelled of the ocean too as if he'd just walked out of it.

When the song stopped, he stopped.

"There'll be another song starting," I said, desperate for whatever this was not to end. I barely knew the guy, and yet, the last five minutes of my life constituted the most exciting time I'd ever spent.

He shook his head, the corners of his lips rising slightly before he moved in to kiss me again. My heart nearly jumped out of my chest as his lips touched mine for a second time. It felt as though I was drowning in him. I gave into the sensation completely.

And then he was gone. I'd not even noticed I'd closed my eyes, but when I opened them, he was nowhere to be seen. I looked along the rocky shore to my left and right, but the promenade was empty. It was only when I looked out to the ocean that I saw him. He was silhouetted against the light of the moon, standing on the rocks about fifty feet in front of me. I wanted to call out to him, to follow him, but he was taking his clothes off. As I watched, he peeled the last item of clothing off, folded it neatly, and dived headlong into the water.

I stepped out onto the first rock, trying to get to him, but my high heels were no match for the slippery algae and seaweed. I looked out into the calm sea, but he had already disappeared from sight.

Behind me, I thought I heard someone in the shadows. A small noise—a cough—gave them away; but when I turned, there was no one there.

The shock

After spending a good five minutes searching the surface of the sea, waiting for him to reappear, it became apparent that he wasn't going to. He'd literally taken his clothes off, jumped into the ocean, and disappeared. It was the second time he'd done that to me now. I couldn't understand why he'd done such a thing. Who leaves a party to go for a swim, and without their clothes, nonetheless? I could still see the outline of his tuxedo on the distant rocks. Behind me, someone called my name, making me jump. I had to get back to the party quickly before anyone realized I'd come down to the water's edge. My parents would kill me if they knew. I took the stairs two at a time, trying not to trip over my gown, and managed to get back up to the balcony just as my mother stuck her head out of the door.

"There you are," she beamed, heading over to me. I gripped the railing tightly, regaining my composure and trying not to show how out of breath I was.

Thankfully, the guard kept quiet about what he'd just seen.

Twinkling lights on the balcony that had been put there for my birthday celebration reflected in her eyes. For a second, I wondered if that's what I'd seen in the stranger's eyes, but then I remembered the lights didn't extend down to the lower level.

"I came out for a little fresh air," I lied. "It looked so pretty with the moon out."

"Yes, it is beautiful tonight," she replied with a distracted air. "Will you come inside? You are missing your own birthday party!"

Taking a deep breath, I looked back out over the ocean. Calm waves lapped at the rocky ocean edge. Half a mile to the left, past the docks, the rocks turned into a beach where people liked to spend their time on sunny days. But here, the ocean was met entirely with rugged coastline. The same rocky coastline I'd loved all my life. "I'll be in soon. I'm just enjoying the solitude."

She laughed her tinkly laugh. The one she never used in public, but I often heard when we were alone together in the palace. "Solitude? It's your big day, and you are missing it."

"Please, mom." It was rare I called her something as informal as mom. I'd been schooled to call her Your Highness in public and mother in private. Still, I didn't want to go back inside, knowing that I might never see him again. I had to know where he'd gone. Ever since I'd first seen him, I'd known he was something special and now... well, now, he was an enigma on top of all that. A puzzle to be solved. I had to know what had happened to him.

"Ok," she gave in. She hugged me close to her. "I just want to let you know how proud I am of you. You looked beautiful in there, dancing with Hayden tonight. You two make a wonderful couple."

I sighed. My mother had wanted me to date Hayden ever since we were little. She often told me stories about how we played together as infants while our mothers gossiped and took high tea. "We aren't a couple. You know he's dating Astrid Farraday."

She made a pssh sound and waved her hand dismissively. "Oh, that's just a silly crush. It won't last long. She's a pretty girl, but not a match for you. Why would he want to date a commoner when he can have a princess? Maybe you should go back in there and dance with him again? Then he'll see what he's missing."

"She's hardly a commoner. Her parents have a high standing in Trifork, and she attended the same exclusive private school as Hayden and I. Besides, don't you think it's a bit classist to call her that?"

I knew she'd never use that particular phrase in public. I was quite surprised to hear her use it in private if I was going to be honest.

"You know what I mean. She's not going to be queen one day is she?"

I shook my head and made a clucking sound with my tongue. "I think he likes her because she's beautiful, kind, intelligent..." I could have come up with another thousand ways to describe her, but I could see my mother had stopped paying attention.

"She's got nothing on you, dear." She moved a stray lock from my face and tucked it behind my ear.

I didn't want to have to tell her that it wasn't like that between Hayden and me. Not again. I'd already had this conversation with her many times in the past, and it was beginning to get boring. He was dating Astrid because I didn't want to date him. I was pretty sure that after about eighth grade, he wasn't interested in me that way either. In fact, we'd had plenty of opportunities to date each other before Astrid entered the picture, and we hadn't taken them. I could understand my mother being eager for me to date and to date someone who came from a family as well respected as the Harrington-Blythes, but she was barking up the wrong tree as far as Hayden and I were concerned.

I rolled my eyes at her.

"I know, I know, he's just a friend." She didn't raise her fingers and make quotation marks in the air with them, but she may as well have. "Just don't take too long out here. Your father and I want to give you your surprise."

She kissed my cheek and wandered back inside, leaving me to dwell on the stranger once more. It was true that I'd never really dated anyone. I think a lot of people had imagined that Hayden and I would eventually get together and at some point in the past, I'd probably thought about it idly myself. But the truth was, I didn't think about it enough. I'd thought more about the stranger in the past few days than I ever thought of Hayden in that way.

I paused and took one more look out onto the ocean. He had gone completely, and for the life of me, I didn't know where. It was like he'd just disappeared into thin air. All I could think was that he'd swam along the shoreline and jumped up on some of the rocks further down. I just couldn't imagine why.

I turned and headed back inside, perplexed. The last song was coming to a close, and the dancers were lining up against the walls, thanks to some of the palace pages, who were ushering people back. The orchestra lowered their instruments as my parents took to a raised platform at the end of the great hall.

"What's happening?" I whispered to Hayden, whom I'd just noticed taking upa place by the door.

"Not sure," he whispered back. "Your father stopped the orchestra and asked for everyone's attention."

This must have been the surprise that my mother was talking about. I'd hoped for something discrete, like a puppy with a ribbon tied around its neck, but I could see that whatever it was, discrete was not something that could be applied to it. I could have done with a little heads up so I could prepare a speech.

"Erica, darling, could you come over here, please?" My mother beckoned me to the raised platform on which the royal thrones were placed. They currently sat empty as both my parents were standing, waiting for me to join them.

"Oh, and Hayden, please come up here too."

All eyes turned to where we were standing.

Hayden looked at me in surprise, and I shrugged. Just next to him, Astrid looked awkward, and I could completely understand why. Hayden spent so much time with me because of our parents' friendship, and it was often noted by the people around us, not to mention the Trifork media, that Hayden and I would make a good couple. Astrid was usually ok with our closeness, knowing that we were more like brother and sister to each other than anything else, but to have us both brought up to the stage at the same time at such an important occasion, well, I could understand why she wasn't thrilled at this sudden scenario. As Hayden stepped towards the raised platform, I grabbed hold of Astrid's hand as a last second thought and brought her with me. She was a good friend of mine and Hayden's girlfriend. If my parents wanted to hand me a present with my friends beside me, Astrid should be included.

I stepped up to the platform just behind Hayden. My mother walked toward me and leaned in. I thought for a second that she was going to whisper something in my ear, but when I looked, she'd bypassed me completely and was talking in hushed tones to Astrid.

Astrid let go of my hand and headed back into the crowd quickly. If I wasn't mistaken, she had tears in her eyes. What was going on? Lord and Lady Harrington-Blythe hurried to the other side of the stage. Hayden looked just as confused as I was at his parents being on stage with us, but they were best friends with my parents, and I had known them since birth, so I guess it made sense. I wondered if they'd helped buy me a present. Lord Harrington-Blythe was the Admiral of the navy. Maybe he'd arranged to replace the ship that had sunk. Thoughts of the captain and crew of the *Erica Rose* came to mind. They still hadn't been found, and it was looking unlikely they ever would be. My heart felt heavy with pain, knowing that the ship could be so replaceable. I knew I'd wanted my own boat. It had been my lifelong dream, but to get another so soon after everything that had happened seemed tacky. I looked down into the crowd to see Anthony grinning up at me from below. Now that Hayden and I had come to the stage, the guests had moved in around the platform. Hundreds of eyes looked up at us expectantly, making me feel nervous. I tried to remember any one of my parents' hank you speeches. They'd given enough of them in the past, and it looked like I was going to be called upon to give one now. Why was it that all words had left me when I needed them the most?

"Thank you all for coming here today to celebrate Erica's eighteenth birthday," my father boomed out, placing his arm over my shoulder. "As you know, the past week has been difficult for us, and especially for Erica, but we've prepared something for her that will make up for it. For those of you that don't know, Erica was involved in an accident with her new ship a couple of days ago. She almost drowned; but as you can see, she is fit and well enough to be here with us today."

My father grinned broadly as the hundreds of people broke out into a round of applause. He waited for the noise to die down before he spoke again.

"Now that Erica is eighteen, she will increase her studies to become a ruler of Trifork, to take over when it is her time. I have every faith that she will do a magnificent job when the time comes. However, the queen and I don't want her to enter into this alone. I was blessed to enter into kinghood with the queen already by my side. Now, I don't expect to be dropping off this mortal coil any day soon, but I'm not getting any younger, and as a nation, we need to be prepared for any eventuality. Erica needs to be prepared to take up my mantle when she succeeds to the throne."

I noticed my mother pushing Hayden forward.

"It is with this in mind, that I'd like to announce the engagement of our daughter, the princess, Erica, to Sir Hayden Harrington-Blythe."

I looked over to Hayden. The shock in his eyes mirrored my own.

No going back

I could barely hear myself think over the rapturous applause. In front of me, all I could see were the happy faces of our guests, excited to be a witness to the royal announcement. At the back of the room, I saw a flash of yellow disappearing out of the main doors as Astrid took off.

"Excuse me," I mumbled, jumping down from the platform and cutting through the crowd. Behind me, I heard my father shouting my name, but I ignored it. I'd be in trouble later, but right now, I didn't care. The doors at the back of the great hall led to an entrance hall and to the large double-sized doors that were the main doors to the palace. One was open. I ran towards it and looked out. Astrid was running down the long driveway to the main gates, her yellow dress flapping about behind her as she ran.

Kicking my shoes off, I pelted down the stairs onto the drive towards her. Beneath my feet, small stones that made up the driveway cut into my soft flesh, but I didn't slow down. Astrid was slightly taller than me and had longer legs, but she was also wearing five-inch heels. I caught up with her about a hundred feet from the main gates. Outside, hundreds of people had turned up to get a glimpse of royalty. There were always people outside with cameras, but because of my birthday and the fact that many of my guests were famous, there were more people outside than usual, desperate to see us.

Astrid glared at me as hundreds of flashes lit up the night thanks to all the people's cameras. I grabbed her arm and pulled her into the gardens. The last thing either of us needed was to become front-page news on top of everything else. She pulled against me, full of anger; but I gripped harder, pulling her across the perfectly manicured lawn between the flower beds. I needed to get her to the grotto, a small opening cut roughly into stone that my great-grandfather had put there in case my great-grandmother got caught in the rain.

The grotto was nothing more than an opening like a man-made cave hewn into rock that backed onto the tall red-bricked walls that surrounded the palace grounds. Inside, a bench took up most of the space. It pointed outwards and in the daytime gave a great view of the gardens. To the side of the bench was a hollow dip, which was full of water. At one side, a pump brought water in, and to the other, a little decorative waterfall fell into a grate in the floor. I used to throw pennies in there as a child and make a wish as one would do to a wishing well. My wish was always the same—to be allowed to go out to sea. Tonight, my only wish was for this all to be a nightmare to wake up from.   Once we were there, away from prying eyes, I pulled Astrid to face me.

"How could you," she spat. I'd never once seen her angry. She was always so sweet. Mind you, she certainly had every right to be.

"It's not happening," I said, trying to calm her down. We were quite far away from the crowds out front, but it was possible that anyone behind the large garden wall could hear us if we talked too loudly. "I don't know what my parents are thinking, but there is no way Hayden and I are getting engaged. It's ludicrous."

"I always knew that there was something between the two of you. Everyone warned me, but Hayden kept telling me you were just friends. I'm such an idiot."

She broke down in tears, falling to the bench behind us. Her whole body heaved with wracking sobs. They'd only been dating for a few months. I knew they liked each other, but I hadn't known just how serious it was.

I sat down next to her and placed my arm around her shoulder, expecting her to shrug me off. She didn't. Maybe she didn't even notice it was there.

"Hayden wasn't lying to you," I said, keeping my voice low. "I can promise you that neither of us knew it was coming. This isn't something we've been hiding behind your back. I have no idea what our parents are playing at, but they kept this a secret from us too. Hayden and I are just friends. You didn't see the shock on his face as my father announced our... the engagement."

She flinched as I said the word engagement, but at least, she was looking at me now.

"You didn't see the shock in mine either. You were too busy running for the door, but I can promise you now, neither of us knew what my father was going to say."

Tears shimmered in her eyes, reflecting the low moonlight and lights of the palace. "You really didn't know?"

"How long have we known each other?" I asked her. "Ten years?"

"Thirteen. We met in kindergarten," she sniffed.

"Thirteen years," I conceded. "We've been friends for a long time. Not once in all that time have I lied to you. I promise that there is nothing, nor has there ever been anything between Hayden and I. I'm not interested in him that way, and I can tell you now that since the pair of you have been dating, he's done nothing but gush about you. He really likes you."

She raised her eyes at me expectantly. "He does?"

"He really does, and as soon as this ridiculous birthday party is over, I'm going to tell my parents that I have no intention of marrying Hayden. I really don't know what they were thinking. My mother kept hinting that we'd make a good couple, but I never expected her to do something like this. She's wrong too. Hayden and I would make a lousy couple. I know him too well. He used the word groovy earlier." I shuddered at the thought of it, making Astrid laugh.

She gave me a small smile. "I'm sorry I was so angry with you. I thought..."

"I know, don't worry about it. I'd have been angry in your position too. Do you want to come back up to the house with me and we'll

71

both drink too much champagne and behave in a very unladylike manner?"

She didn't have time to answer because just then, a number of guards with flashlights made their way across the garden. The beam of one caught us.

"His Majesty requests your presence inside," announced one of the guards.

I stood and helped Astrid to her feet.

"Not her," instructed the guard. "I've been ordered to escort her home."

I was just about to give him a piece of my mind when I saw my father dashing over to us. His face was as dark as thunder.

"You'd better go home," I whispered glumly to Astrid. "I'll sort all of this out and speak to you later."

She nodded and left with the guard. My father grabbed me roughly by the arm, making me cry out in pain.

"What are you doing?" I yelled, trying to pull away from him.

"Don't talk to me," he hissed. Back in the palace, he finally let me go in one of the small rooms away from the entrance hall.

"You embarrassed me out there," he yelled. "How dare you just walk out like that? You've made us a laughing stock!"

My father rarely got angry, and it was scary to see him like this. I wasn't about to back down though. What they had done was ludicrous.

I opened my mouth to retaliate when my mother walked in. I turned to her for help, but she walked over to my father's side.

"What were you thinking, Erica?" she asked. I could see the disappointment in her eyes.

Were they kidding? What right did they have to be angry and disappointed in me after what they'd done?

I pulled myself up to my full height, placing my hands on my hips. "I left because you'd announced I was going to be married," I yelled. "You want to know what I was thinking? I was thinking how insane it was that my parents told an entire room full of people that I was to be married without even consulting me first."

My voice had become shrill, and I didn't even care. I didn't wait for a response; I left the room, slamming the door behind me and ran up the back stairs to my bedroom where I slammed that door too for good measure.

I don't think I'd ever been so angry in my life. I picked up a pillow and threw it across the room. It missed the wall and went right through my French windows that led out onto my balcony.

Seconds later, my mother entered the room. That was the worst thing about being a princess. Privacy wasn't a luxury I was afforded, and because of that, there was no lock on the door.

"I'm sorry we've upset you," she began, taking a seat on my bed. She patted the bed beside her, inviting me to sit. I stayed where I was beside my dresser. I tried to ignore the photo of Hayden and I that had been taken a couple of years ago and that I'd tucked into the frame of the mirror.

"I honestly thought you'd be happy," she said with no hint of irony.

"Happy?" I asked incredulously. "You announced I was to be married. Married!" I repeated it figuring it deserved to be.

My mother clucked. "Yes, I know it's big, but we've joked for years that the pair of you would end up married."

I huffed in exasperation. "Joked, yes, exactly! I never disputed it, because that's all it was, a joke. The punch line is turning out to be not very funny. What does Hayden think of all this anyway?"

"I don't exactly know. When you ran out, I was more concerned about you. Your father asked everyone to leave at that point, so he's probably gone home with his parents."

"He's going to be so angry. He's dating Astrid. You know that. We had a discussion about it less than an hour ago outside, remember?"

"Yes," she conceded, getting up from her place on the bed. She took a step toward me. "I remember, but she'll get over it. They've only been dating for what? A couple of months? Three at most."

"That's not the point, though," I said backing away from her. If she was coming toward me for a hug, she was going to be sorely disappointed. "Even if he wasn't dating Astrid, I still wouldn't want to marry him."

She sighed. "He's a good catch, Erica."

"I didn't catch him, though, did I? He's been thrust upon me. I'm eighteen years old. There is plenty of time for me to marry. Why does it have to be now, and why does it have to be with Hayden?"

Not that I had anything against Hayden. I wasn't ready to marry anyone, certainly not someone I wasn't in love with. I'd never known falling in love. It was not something I'd remotely felt for Hayden. The closest thing I'd felt to it was outside just half an hour previously when my heart had been hammering so loudly that I was worried people would be able to hear it. The stranger had taken my breath away completely. I didn't know if it was love. I'd only just met him, but I knew it was a lot closer to it than anything I'd ever felt for Hayden.

My mother sighed and began again as if her keeping talking would somehow change my mind. "You've got a history. You've been friends for as long as I can remember. Your father wants you to have someone to help you, to take this journey with you so when you do eventually become queen, you won't be alone. He trusts Hayden, you like Hayden. The question should be, why shouldn't it be Hayden? Who better to help you rule Trifork?"

I thought back to my mysterious stranger. Funnily enough, marriage didn't seem so ludicrous when he was in my mind. I shrugged the thought off. I didn't even know the guy's name, and here I was picturing him as my groom. Up until about an hour ago, I'd not thought about marriage at all. I was only eighteen. There was plenty of time for it. I'd always pictured myself sailing the ocean before settling down.

"I don't want to marry Hayden," I reiterated, sitting down on the bed. "I don't love him in that way."

"I'm sorry. You are right," my mother conceded. "We shouldn't have sprung this on you. We wanted it to be a lovely surprise for your birthday. I honestly thought you'd be happy. I know you've always had a soft spot for Hayden, and his parents were thrilled when we put the idea to them.

"They knew you were going to announce this?" I asked, folding my arms.

"Of course, they did. We could hardly marry their son off without even telling them."

My eyes widened at the ridiculousness of what she was saying. "But you were happy to do it without telling him...or me?"

"I've already apologized for that. It was unwise, and I'm deeply sorry for upsetting you. We shouldn't have announced your engagement without asking you first. Can we chalk it up to one big silly mistake and forget it ever happened?"

I heaved a sigh of relief. "Of course. Thank you."

"Good," She replied, jumping up from the bed. "I'm glad we are friends again. It's getting late. You should probably get some sleep. It's been a long night."

The last few days had been a maelstrom of things for me to deal with, and I was exhausted. The painkillers I'd taken earlier had worn off, and both my side and my head were beginning to hurt again. I pulled off the dress and got into my pajamas before dropping onto the bed.

I stifled a yawn as I watched my mother retrieve my ball gown from the floor. "What will you tell the guests? About the engagement being off I mean?"

She shook her head quickly. "When I said it was a silly mistake, I meant the announcement. The engagement is still going ahead. I've just had my secretary book the catering. You'll be marrying Hayden in three months' time."

Dragged in

If being engaged wasn't bad enough, the media excitement that followed was a complete nightmare. I'd hoped that once I turned eighteen, I'd have more freedom, but now that my engagement had been announced, it was impossible to leave the palace through the front gates. Hundreds of photographers camped out there every day and night. The only way to go outside without being spotted was either to go onto the private balcony from my bedroom or to go to the private area out back that led down to the sea. We owned about two hundred meters of shoreline which was fenced off at both ends. To the left of our property line were the docks and then the public beach. To the right, was moorland that ended in sheer cliffs that fell away to the sea. The back of the palace was the only place I was allowed to go by myself and the only place I got some peace and quiet.

I'd spent the best part of a week trying to persuade my parents to change their minds about the wedding, but it seemed the more I pleaded, the more resolute they became. Over a thousand invitations had been sent out, the catering had been booked, and the media had been told the official date. I'd been asked to give a short interview with a reporter but had absolutely refused, so my parents had done it instead. I hadn't seen it on the TV, but I could imagine what they said.

As I stepped out to the walkway, one of the guards came forward to follow me as they always did. Shooting him a sharp look, I walked right past him.

"I'm eighteen now. I don't need to be watched anymore. I'm not a child."

He looked at me uncertainly but backed off. I had a plan, and the last thing I needed was to be watched. I'd dressed in sensible footwear. Heels would be no use for what I was planning. I headed down to the paved promenade and pretended to take a stroll, walking slowly. I had a book with me, not to read but to give the impression I was going to. Once I'd walked far enough so the guard could no longer see me, I dropped it on the low wall that separated the rocks from the promenade and jumped over.

The rocks were slightly drier than they had been the night of the ball, thanks to the baking sun, but I still had to watch out for bits of seaweed. Out in the distance, I could still see the tuxedo that the stranger had left. It had been there nearly a week, and by some miracle, no one had spotted it, and the tide hadn't taken it out to sea. Grey rocks surrounded small rock pools filled with sea anemones and crabs. I stepped over each one, being careful not to lose my balance.

As I got closer to the stranger's clothes, I saw the reason his suit was still there. He'd wedged it under a particularly heavy rock at the high tide mark. I tried picking the rock up, pulling it, pushing it. I even tried kicking it to no avail. The stranger must have been immensely strong to be able to pick up a rock this size to put his clothes under.

I sat on the rock and gazed out to sea. It was especially calm with only slight ripples lapping at my feet. Glancing around to make sure no one was watching, I pulled my shoes off and dipped my feet in the cool water. On a summer's day, especially one as hot as it was, the feeling of the salt water on my feet was heavenly.

Even though the water barely reached my ankles, the terrifying thought that something bad would happen lingered, thanks to years of being told how dangerous the sea was, not to mention my near-death experience only a week before.

I let my hand trail down to feel the fabric of the jacket below me. It had been almost a week since I'd last seen him. A week I'd spent locked in my room, hiding away from the world, sitting on my balcony searching for him. Just like the first time I saw him, he'd come from nowhere and gone back there.

I sighed wistfully. In the eighteen years I'd been on the planet, meeting him was the most exciting thing that had ever happened to me, and it was over. Whatever it was that had happened between us, which admittedly wasn't much, had come to an end.

Between my fingers, something crinkled. I pressed it again and looked down. There was something in the jacket pocket. I slipped my fingers between the folds of fabric and pulled out a piece of thin plastic. When I looked closely, I saw it was actually a note written on paper and slipped inside a transparent folder to keep the moisture out. It only said one word. *Midnight.*

My heart pounded as I took in the note. I turned it over, hoping to see something else on the back, but it was blank. The paper itself looked like it had been torn from the edge of a newspaper. I could just make out a couple of letters of newsprint on the edge. The writing was scruffy, almost as if a child had written it, and yet, I knew it was his writing. It was strange how someone as well dressed as he was would write so scruffily, but that only added to the enigma that was him.

Midnight. Was this note meant for me or just something he had in his pocket? Another puzzle. It had been almost a week since my party. Six midnights had come and gone since he'd left this note. I folded it as best I could and put it into my pocket, excitement fizzing through me.

I had a lead. Ok, I had no way of knowing if the note was for me, or if I'd already missed my chance, but one thing I did know was that I was going to be down on these rocks at midnight tonight.

Leaving the clothes behind, I headed back to the palace, being careful to keep out of the eye line of the guard on the back entrance of the palace. I'd barely made it over the low wall onto the promenade when I heard my mother calling me.

"Erica, dear, there you are. I've been searching all over the palace for you. Your father and I need to talk to you." I looked up to find her peering over the balcony. With a sigh, I started up the stairs, ready for the fight that I'd left stewing for days.

"There is no way in a million years I'm going to marry Hayden," I snapped, before offering either of my parents the chance to say otherwise. I'd barely spoken to them in the past few days. Instead, keeping to my room and purposely staying clear of the pair of them.

We were sitting in my father's private study, a room full of rich leather chairs and paintings of men on horseback hunting for foxes. When I say sitting, my father was sitting, I was standing by the door, ready to make my escape and my mother paced the floor with the same impatient air she always wore. She always looked like she had someplace more important to be and was desperate to be there. Her arms were folded across her chest, her face set in a grimace. Clearly, she wasn't looking forward to this conversation any more than I was. My father, on the other hand, looked as he always did. Detached, stoic. You could never quite tell what he was thinking which was a great way to be for the leader of a kingdom, but crappy as a trait for a father.

"I don't see the problem," my father said, twirling one thumb around the other. "He's a nice enough boy. You are always with him anyway. This way, it will save him the trip from his house to the palace."

I could scarcely believe what I was hearing. Saving him on shoe leather was hardly a good reason to marry. "I don't love him. He's dating my friend for goodness sake."

"Yes, well your mother assured me that it wasn't serious between them."

"It isn't," she interrupted, turning and strolling in the other direction. If this conversation went on much longer, she'd wear a path in the carpet.

My father cleared his throat. "Anyway, as I said at the ball, you will ascend to the throne one day, and it's going to be much easier with someone by your side. I can't imagine having to do it alone.

I placed my hands on the desk in front of him and looked him straight in the eye.

"I'd rather become a queen on my own than drag someone who doesn't love me and that I don't love into a marriage that neither of us wants. You promised me that once I became eighteen, you would start teaching me everything I needed to know about ruling a kingdom. I'm eighteen now, Daddy, and I'm willing to learn, but until I find someone I love, who loves me, I will not be getting married."

My father sighed and slumped slightly in his chair. "I thought that was what you would want. I assumed that Hayden, being who he is would be a bonus for you. You always loved the sea, what better than to marry a sea captain?"

I arched a brow, not quite understanding what he was talking about. "Sea captain?"

"Of course! His father is the Admiral of the Royal Fleet. Of course, he's going to be a sea captain. You know, if you two became man and wife, he would probably let you go on his ship with him."

It was a bribe of the worst kind. Mainly, because he knew that sailing around the world with Hayden would be a dream come true, for me anyway. Hayden had never shown much interest in becoming a sea captain, despite his father's position. He loved sailing, it was responsibility that was his problem.

I paused, mulling it over in my mind. Would living with Hayden as his wife be such a bad thing? We were best friends and already spent a lot of time together, so I knew we were compatible. He was good-looking too if you were into that sort of thing. Cute, too cute for his own good, really, like an oversized puppy, with large brown eyes and a constant cheeky grin on his face. Yes, I could do a lot worse than waking up every day on our very own ship, sailing to far and distant lands rather than being stuck under the scrutiny of the media and the adoring public of Trifork. Astrid would be upset for a while, but she'd understand...eventually. I tried to talk myself into it as it seemed my mother and father were not about to be talked out of it any time soon.

"I'll think about it," I huffed, turning towards the door. I saw my mother give a satisfied smirk as I left the room.

It was all I thought about as I headed to my room. Was it possible to fall in love with a friend? Someone I'd known for my whole life. Hayden was certainly loveable, but I wasn't in love with him. I wished he was here so I could talk the whole thing through with him. There was every chance that he didn't know he was being made a sea captain and getting his own ship. I got the feeling it was something my father made up in the heat of the moment to entice me to change my mind.

I was still contemplating a life with Hayden as I headed out onto my balcony. I'd spent so much time out here that I knew every rock and the shape of the coastline heading off into the distance. Tonight, I was looking for something that wasn't familiar to me at all. Tonight, I wasn't just going to be looking at the coastline and rocks, I was going to be down there. The clock moved so slowly, and the sun took even longer to set than it usually did, or at least, it felt that way. I whiled away the time planning my route to the water's edge. Thankfully, the moon was out again, although not as bright as it had been. There was no way I'd be able to get past the guards downstairs without being spotted, so when midnight was almost upon me, I climbed over the balcony railings to my parents adjoining balcony and used the fire escape there.

Finding a safe route over the rocks was almost impossible. The moon kept disappearing behind clouds, rendering me almost blind. I took each step slowly, speeding up a little each time the moon peeked through and hoping that I wasn't going to be late for whatever it was that happened at midnight.

The sea was at high tide, and the waves had picked up slightly. The clothes were still lodged under the rocks where they had been for the past week, but now, they were being dampened by sea spray. Looking around me, I couldn't see anything except the distant beam of the lighthouse on the horizon to my right.

Now that I was here, all bravado left me. I was getting wetter by the second and dangerously close to falling into the tumultuous sea. I couldn't see the hands on my watch in the darkness, but I was pretty sure it was already past midnight. I was just about to turn around and head back to the palace when a hand appeared from below the inky surface and dragged me in.

Underneath

Panic gripped me as the freezing water surrounded me. Above me, the surface thrashed and foamed, and yet, the water dulled my sense of hearing to almost silence. It was so dark, I couldn't see, and without my senses working properly, I couldn't tell which way was up. I closed my eyes, trying to concentrate on making my way to the surface, trying to figure a way out of this. Because of my mother's fear of the ocean, a fear I was beginning to understand, considering that this was the second time in a week I was drowning, I'd never learned to swim. Not even in a swimming pool. I'd seen other people do it and had a general idea, but as I kicked my legs about, I knew it was having no effect. I thrashed my arms around, desperate to break the surface to breathe, but I was so disoriented and panicked, that I made no progress. The hand that pulled me in was still holding me, dragging me further down towards the ocean floor, or at least, I assumed that's where we were heading. I wanted to open my mouth to scream, but I knew that if I did, it would only let in the sea water which would flow down to my lungs, causing me to drown in the most horrible manner.

"Calm down." A man's voice came through the water, and yet, I didn't hear it with my ears, the words came directly to my brain. It was him. I recognized the strange way he spoke, even though now, he wasn't actually using his mouth to speak at all. My mind was playing tricks on me. I'd heard that in a person's last dying seconds, their mind can make them believe things that aren't real, and I wondered if this was what was happening to me now. I was dying, and in my final moments of life, I was hearing words underwater.

"You're not dying," said the voice, which only confirmed to me that I must be. He could hear my thoughts now as well as putting words into my head.

I opened my eyes. The salt water stung them, and I still couldn't see anything beyond the bubbles I was creating with my writhing body.

The hand gripped my arm more tightly and began pulling me through the water. This time we were going at high speed. Water rushed past me so quickly that the fear of drowning was overcome by the fear of crashing into something. What was going on? What was it that was propelling us through the water? I'd not seen a boat out on the ocean but being pulled along by one was the only explanation I could think of. I closed my eyes one more time, to shield them from the fast-paced water and let myself be pulled to wherever it was that we were going, not that I had any choice in the matter.

After a good ten minutes or so, we slowed down. The water was warmer here, or at least I didn't feel the cold as much as I had when I'd first been pulled in.

"*Open your eyes.*" The voice came again as we came to a stop and again it wasn't spoken, just an echo in my head.

"*Open them,*" he repeated softly. I noticed he'd let go of my arm.

I blinked a few times before realizing we were in a cave. A huge underwater cave filled with water.

I opened my mouth to speak, but as I did, the salt water filled it.

"*Talk with your mind,*" the stranger said, but it was too late, I could taste the saltiness of the water that burned as it went down my throat. I began to panic again, but the stranger wrapped his arm around my waist and swam with me upwards. Cold air hit my face, disorienting me as we finally hit the surface.

The only light in the cavern came from a small hole in the ceiling above us. About the size of a jam jar lid, it was not big enough to crawl through, but it let in just enough moonlight for me to see the stranger in front of me.

I took in a deep breath and promptly began to choke, coughing up the seawater that had filled my lungs when I'd tried talking just moments before. A small sandy beach sloped gradually out from the water, but overhead, rocks told me we were still in a cave. A cave where the only way out was through a tunnel under the water. The air was thin, but breathable, although it smelled like it could do with a good gust of wind to rid it of its fishy smell. I wrinkled up my nose as the stranger hauled me to the shore, leaving me half in and half out of the water and finally allowing me to get a good look at him again. I thought I remembered how beautiful he was, but now that I saw him again, I realized that I'd not done him justice with my memory of him. His skin, almost blue in the sliver of pale moonlight that accentuated the deep muscles of his chest, dripped with sea water. I watched rivulets of salty ocean water roll down over his stomach before dripping into the sand below him. It was so distracting, that, not for the first time, I felt flustered around him.

He waited until I'd finished coughing up half the ocean before speaking.

"How are you?" A small sliver of moonlight danced across the surface of the water creating a strange light show across the cave behind him.

Indignation filled me, despite my awkwardness around him. It made me feel better, knowing that I could feel something other than a powerful attraction to him that almost scared me. That, in and of itself, was dangerous. Dangerous and wholly the most exciting emotion I'd ever felt. A little indignation would help me drown it out a little.

"How am I?" I croaked, trying to get the words out despite my throat now feeling like I'd emptied a salt cellar into it.

He looked at me strangely then, those green eyes of his sparkling in the moonlight with not a hint of purple to them. It was almost as though he was surprised by my outburst, but he recovered quickly from whatever it was that had surprised him. He nodded his head to my question. I coughed fiercely, annoyed that I couldn't shout at him as I wanted to. My raspy voice could barely get above a whisper, thanks to me consuming half the ocean. "How do you think I am? You came to my party, left without saying a word and then tried to drown me when I came to thank you for saving me." You are also making my brain fuzzy with how utterly beautiful you are, and my heart almost hurt with how much I want to touch you. I kept the last two thoughts to myself, hoping he wasn't still poking around in my brain.

He lounged back on the cold sand, lazily grinning at me, a twinkle in his eye.

"Repeat back what you just said." Even though he was communicating with me through his mind, I could still hear the humor in his voice.

"I said I was only on my way to thank you when you tried to murder me by pulling me into the ocean."

I saw his grin widen at the edges. *"Remind me what it was you were going to thank me for when I so rudely tried drowning you."*

"I was going to thank you for saving me from drow..." Realization hit me that what I was about to say sounded ridiculous. Not that it made me any less angry. He'd still pulled me into the ocean and dragged me to goodness knew where.

"You can't drown when you are with me. Haven't you noticed that you are still alive after being underwater more than twenty minutes?

Now, I don't know a lot about humans, but I'm pretty sure that after a couple of minutes down here, they usually drop dead without oxygen."

I eyed him suspiciously. It wasn't helping my concentration much that he was completely naked. At least, his top half was; his bottom half was still under the water line.

I thought back to when he'd pulled me under. Now that he mentioned it, it did seem like a long time to be underwater. Having never been under water for longer than it took to take a sip from my tap to swill out toothpaste, I wasn't exactly sure how long a person could survive below the surface, but remembering how awful it felt almost drowning the previous week, I figured it couldn't have been long.

So, the question remained, why hadn't I just drowned?

"What did you do? Secret oxygen tanks?" I looked around me on the underground beach to see if there was any kind of scuba equipment lying around. All I saw was a starfish lapping at the waterline and a crab scuttling across the sand.

"I think you might have noticed if I put a mask on you," he drawled, his inner voice smoother than chocolate. I wished he'd talk properly so I could hear what it really sounded like. His lip twitched up at the side as he waited for me to

come to some kind of realization. I just didn't know what it was. I also felt like an idiot around him. If only my heart would slow down a bit so I could think straight.

His confidence annoyed me. Why couldn't I be like that? Most people got nervous at meeting a member of royalty for the first time. The stranger hadn't even had the decency to bow to me. I've spent my life being schooled to be polite, to have confidence around strangers, but with him, all that went out of the window. Any princessy politeness was forgotten as I tried to think what to say next. He was so distracting, lying there, a self-assured smile on his face. I was annoyed, sure, but it was getting more and more difficult to stay that way when my heart was hammering the way it was.

"Ok, smartass, how is it that I've been underwater for so long and not drowned?" I asked loudly, spitting out the last of the salty water. My voice echoed around the chamber, sending the crab scuttling in the other direction. I sat up on the beach and pulled my knees up out of the warm water, hugging them close to me and waited for the remnants of my voice to die out.

"I brought you here because I thought you might like to see this," he replied without answering my question at all. *"Dip your toe into the water."*

I eyed him warily. I'd only just pulled my feet up out of the water.

"Just do it," he urged, an easy smile playing on his lips. I waited about ten seconds before acquiescing to his demand. I didn't want him thinking it was okay for him to boss me around. I let go of my legs and moved one foot forward, inching it to the water's edge. Slowly I let my toe into the water. It was warmer than the air.

I shivered slightly. "It's warm, so what?"

He grinned at me now. This whole thing was just a game to him, and yet, what choice did I have but to play it? There was no other way out as far as I could see. The cave was completely sealed from above, and I couldn't swim back through the tunnel without help. He had me well and truly trapped. I wasn't sure if the thought of it scared me or filled me with excitement. Probably a bit of both.

"I'm not going to keep you here," he growled inside my head and then added, *"Kick the water."*

I kicked out slightly. From around my foot, the water began to glow, a pale blue light that glittered and then evaporated leaving the water black again. My eyes widened in shock, and I quickly pulled my foot back onto dry land.

"It's phosphorescence," he explained, putting his hand into the water and clapping the surface so it glimmered around him for a few seconds. *"Movement in the water causes it to light up."* When he was still the surface of the water turned back to inky blackness.

"It's beautiful," I exclaimed, bringing my foot down into the water, splashing the pair of us.

"You haven't seen anything yet," he said with a grin and rolled back into the water. His head disappeared under the tranquil surface before he began to swim. The way he swam was unrefined, peculiar for someone who'd I'd begun to associate with the sea. But as the water bubbled around his flailing body, I realized what he was doing. He was churning the water. With each rough stroke, the water glowed more until the whole cave was lit up as though a thousand fairy lights had been turned on. Below water below the surface was now transformed. What I'd assumed would be nothing but sand and rocks was really a secret underwater garden with hundreds of underwater plants, each of them lit up with the motion of the water. Thousands of beautiful fish swam through delicate coral, making me want to dive back down to touch them.

The stranger did a lap around the whole cave before ending up right back where he started, lazily gliding through the water in front of me.

The cave glimmered and glittered all around us, magically illuminated by the phosphorescence on the water's surface, and light danced over the stranger's body, slowly dimming as he pulled himself up onto the beach beside me. I sighed at the fleeting beauty of it. Already it was starting to fade, and I knew that within a minute, the water would go back to the appearance of lifelessness and we would be once more plunged into darkness.

As the last bit of light extinguished, I turned back to the stranger, eager to let him know just how beautiful I'd found it. He'd moved down the beach slightly, so that he was right next to me. I trailed my eyes down his wet body and stopped in shock. There, where his legs should be, he had a tail. My stranger was a mermaid.

The Merman

"Merman," he corrected me. I hadn't even spoken. I was too busy being in shock to use my mouth for actual words. He was reading the thoughts right from my head again. I had to keep them reigned in.

I tensed up, holding in the scream I wanted to make and, instead, opted for a few deep breaths as I tried to come to terms with what I was seeing in front of me. I would have passed it off as a trick of the light had there been much light in the dim cave.

"You're not real," I pointed out as if stating the obvious. I pulled myself away from him, scared that I was completely losing my mind. "Mermaids are fairytale creatures."

If he was offended that I was denying his existence, he didn't act it.

"All stories start off with a kernel of truth. Giant is just another name for an unusually large person, and witch is a term for someone who makes potions. Don't pharmacists do that?"

I shook my head before meeting his eyes and holding his gaze. "Giants and witches are people, though. They don't have fish tails." My voice was echoing again, but I didn't care. I was trapped in an underwater cave with a half man-half fish.

"I'm not a half fish," he replied indignantly, *"although I prefer it to you calling me a mermaid. Maid is a woman, man is a ... well, is a man."*

He was listening to my thoughts again.

"Please stop doing that," I snapped, clapping my hands to my ears. He splashed his tail up and down in the water, lighting up the cave around us with each movement in an eerie blue color. I felt my heart rate increase out of fear with each movement he made. Five minutes ago, this whole place and situation had felt romantic. Now it was just alien to me; the creepy lights making fearsome shadows on the cave walls.

"I'm sorry," he replied, leaning toward me. I leaned backward, but not quite far enough. He took hold of my hands and pulled them gently away from my ears. His hands were strong but

delicate as he let them drop by my side. The moonlight illuminated his face, highlighting the cut of his cheekbones, the wetness of his lower lip from the ocean water. His eyes were now purple, and like the salt water to the side of us, they had their own sparkle. I'd thought there was something otherworldly about him when I first saw him, thanks to those eyes, and now, he'd confirmed it. His home was down here, beneath the waves. No wonder I'd thought he was connected to the sea. He was part of it. It was his home.

He put his hand to my face, and slowly traced it up the side of my head letting it rest on my right temple. *"That's how we communicate down here. There's very little sound underwater, and speaking doesn't come easily to me. I should have known you'd be scared."*

Realization hit me. "That's why you didn't speak at my party."

He nodded, lowering his eyes to the sand between us. *"Among other reasons, yes."*

I thought back to the party, how sure of himself he'd looked, cocky even. But now that I remembered it, he had an air of uncertainty about him, like a lost child.

I'd wanted to kiss him then. Even with all my family watching me, with the heads of state of at least five of the nine kingdoms in attendance, not to mention the hundreds of other dignitaries, I'd wanted to lean forward and kiss him. Outside the party on the promenade, I had kissed him, and it had been magical. Now, I wasn't so sure. I felt cold and scared.

He looked up at me in surprise.

Before I thought about why he would look at me that way, he took my hand. *"Please, trust me. I promise I'll take you home. I didn't set out to alarm you, I just wanted..."* he trailed off. There was something in his eyes, something that made me realize that this was just as scary for him as it was for me. All his former bravado had gone along with the flashes of purple in his eyes. They had gone back to the pale green they'd been before.

"I just wanted to get to know you."

I could almost feel his heart beating as he looked at me so earnestly. I couldn't read his mind as he could mine, but in that moment, I knew I was safe. He'd saved my life, he had no reason to hurt me now.

He held his hand out for me, and this time, I took it.

"If you keep hold of my hand, you'll be able to breathe underwater. You'll also be able to see better than you would without me. It's part of the magic we possess."

I let him guide me into the water, no longer feeling nervous. The excitement I'd felt earlier was creeping back.

I stepped into the warm darkness, enjoying the feel of the water as I sank deeper and deeper into its depths. He pulled me close, wrapping an arm around me, so I was crushed up against his chest, with my arm around his back. His skin was so much warmer than my own, and I had to compose myself not to think about how naked he was next to me, not to notice that the skin of my fingers and arm touched him. He swished his tail around to light the water, creating a maelstrom of bubbles around us. As the bubbles cleared, a whole other world emerged, still illuminated by the phosphorescence. Thousands of beautiful fish swam around us, completely unafraid of our presence. I'd seen them from above water, but now that I was among them, I saw how stunningly beautiful they were. Pink and purple coral grew, covering the sandy floor of the cavern, which, in turn, was covered with vibrant sea anemones and colorful fish, dashing in and out, creating a breathtaking scene in front of me.

At least, it would have been breathtaking if I was breathing. With the stranger holding my hand, I didn't need to. I hadn't breathed the whole way here, not in the normal sense; but then, I'd been too panicked to notice. Now, I felt so at ease, weightless in the salty blue water, my senses filled with wonder at this beautiful place. A playful creature swam past, brushing against my arm. I pulled back quickly, nervous, but the stranger laughed. *"Don't mind him, that's just Ollie. He doesn't bite."*

"Ollie?" I replied, this time using my mind to speak to him, confident that he could hear me. The creature came back, and this time I let it come to rest on my hand.

"An octopus. He's kind of a friend of mine. I think you call them pets above land."

An octopus. Such a strange word for a strange creature. He wrapped his legs around my fingers, tickling the palm of my hand.

He unwrapped himself from my hand and darted off, back into the shadows. The light was dimming, so I waved my hand about creating a trail of light.

The blue glow lit up his face as he grinned at me enjoying myself. I'd loved the sea for as long as I could remember, but not in my wildest dreams had I ever imagined something as wonderful as this beneath its depths. I gave the stranger a shy smile now that I'd caught him looking at me. His green eyes crinkled up at the edges. Below the water, the deep shadows of his chest muscles were prominent. I couldn't stop the blush that rose up from my chest. I only hoped the fading blue light hid the redness of my cheeks.

"I should go back," I said in my mind. I didn't want to, I could have happily stayed down here forever, but the light had begun to change. The soft blue of the phosphorescence was now being replaced by the pink tinge of dawn, filtering down from the small holes in the cavern roof. Had we really been down here that long?

The stranger nodded, his long charcoal hair flowing out behind him like obsidian flames, framing his pale face.

He moved closer, putting his arm around my waist to gently guide me through the tunnel until we emerged back out into the open sea. It was much darker here without the phosphorescence, but I could still make out basic shapes thanks to the dawn's early light. The vastness of the ocean astounded me. Okay, I'd seen it from above, but it was a completely different experience down here. It seemed to go on forever in every direction with the seabed below us and the surface above.

The journey back to the rocks couldn't have been more different to the journey from them. Then it had been dark, and I'd been terrified. I was still scared, but now, it was a different kind of scared. It was exciting, new. I looked around me, eager to take everything in before I'd have to leave it to go back to my own world. The fish weren't as concentrated here, but I still saw them as we swam past. Long fish that looked a little like snakes, schools of tiny red fish, swimming as though they were one, large silver fish that I recognized because we sometimes ate them for dinner. Disappointment weighed heavily as the rocks appeared in the distance. I knew I had to go back home and get changed into dry clothes before my parents noticed I was missing, but I didn't want this night to come to an end. The ocean was vast, and I wanted to explore. I wanted to spend more time with the stranger.

"We will have time," he answered my thoughts. *"You know where I am. If I'm close, I'll hear you."* and I knew he meant with his mind. I wished I could hear his thoughts the way he heard mine. Sure, I could hear what he wanted to project out there, but everything else that he was thinking remained a mystery. I couldn't help thinking that it put me at a disadvantage.

"We're here," he observed, pointing out the rocks. All I had to do was to swim to the surface and climb out. I grabbed one of the rocks to pull myself up, but he pulled me back. I turned to face him, wondering what he

wanted, but before I had time to form the question in my mind, his lips were upon mine. In the cold water, his lips felt surprisingly warm as he brought his body closer to me. My mind was ablaze with sensations, none of which I could articulate if I wanted to. I hoped he wasn't trying to probe my thoughts because I could barely make sense of it at all. All I could think was how salty his lips were, how he tasted like the sea, every other thought was obliterated as he crushed his lips hungrily to mine.

"You know where to find me," he said, pulling back. With a swift push up, I breached the surface, taking in a huge breath as I clung to one of the rocks. I looked down to where he'd been, but he was already gone, swum away into the briny depths.

I scrambled up the slippery rocks until I was completely out of the sea. Turning, I gazed out over the waves hoping to spot him again, but all I saw were a couple of gulls overhead and a sailboat in the distance.

I turned back towards the palace, my heart both frizzing with excitement from what had been and heavy, knowing I'd have to wait before experiencing it again—and came face to face with my mother, the queen.

Hayden

"Where have you been?" she demanded, her features contorted in fury, and beneath that, I saw the fear in her eyes. I stood there looking at her, my nightgown dripping wet, clinging to my body. I shivered, partly from the cold and partly under the weight of her stare. I'd committed the worst sin possible in her eyes. All I'd heard my entire childhood was not to go out into the sea. My mother's entire existence it seemed was to keep me away from the water and here I was breaking the cardinal rule. Again!

"I went for a swim," I stammered lamely.

"A swim!" Her voice was harsh. I'd never seen her so angry in my whole life. "Who were you with and don't try telling me no one. I saw a man."

There was no point denying it if she'd seen him. I opened my mouth to tell her, but then I realized he hadn't even told me his name. I'd only thought of him as the stranger, and I could hardly tell her that.

"I thought I'd come down to the rocks and see if I could see the man who saved me from drowning to thank him."

My mother's eyes narrowed suspiciously. "He was just a figment of your imagination. The nurse said so. I don't know who you thought you were with out there, but I'm willing to bet it was someone who was out to harm you. You are a princess, and because of that, you are a target. Now, let's get you home so you can change into some dry clothes."

She grabbed my arm and dragged me back across the rocks to the palace. Without letting go, she hauled me up the stairs to one of the bathrooms where she instructed my maid to fill the bath for me. "I'll come back and talk to you later about this," she fumed, before turning on her heel and stalking out of the room.

I'd seen my mother upset before, but never like this. I looked down to see a hint of a bruise on my arm from where she'd held me. My father was usually the one with the temper, but even then, he only directed it at his enemies— never us. My mother often had a look of disapproval upon her face and knew how to make it clear when she was unhappy about something. But as a queen, she knew how to keep her temper down, until now that was.

Wisps of steam floated up from the bath and Dora, my maid, moved to turn the cold tap on.

"Don't!" I said to her, but she ignored me and turned the tap to cold anyway. I was just about to reprimand her when I realized I'd spoken to her with my mind, the way I'd spent the night speaking to the stranger. I thought back to our conversations, and it dawned on me that I hadn't heard his actual voice once since that day on the beach when he'd saved my life. I'd only heard him inside my head.

Dora laid out a towel for me, curtseyed, and left me alone in the grand bathroom. Usually, I took a bath in the small en-suite off my bedroom, but for whatever reason, my mother had brought me here to the palace's main bathroom. The room itself was huge, with a high ceiling and glimmering tiles covering the floor. The bath, an oversized roll top with silver claw feet stood in the dead center of the room with a chandelier directly overhead. Around the base of the bath, inlaid into the floor, were grates so the water could overflow. I turned off the cold and added more hot water. As soon as the stranger had let go of me, I'd felt cold. It was as though his presence had kept me warm. Perhaps that was also part of the magic he held. I peeled off my dripping nightdress and threw it onto the floor, before sinking right up to my neck in the scalding water. I let out a low moan as heat seeped back into my bones. Turning off the hot tap, I lay back in the water, letting my hair float around me. Closing my eyes, I sank below the surface, holding my breath as I did.

"*Hello,*" I called out in my mind, but there was no answer. Either he had to be closer to me, or I had to be in the ocean for him to hear my thoughts. I opened my eyes and looked up at the chandelier. Its crystals twinkled in the light, throwing rainbows around the room. I didn't want to come back up to the surface. It was as if all my problems left me if I was underwater, but pretty soon, I had to. Without the stranger holding on to me, I needed the oxygen above the surface to be able to breathe.

I washed my hair slowly, using more shampoo than was really required to rid it of all the salt I'd picked up in the ocean. I was in no rush to get out. I knew my mother would be waiting for me so she could shout some more. I looked down at my arm. The bruise was darker now, more defined. I could almost see her fingerprints in it. She'd always had a problem with the sea. The issue she had with the ocean all seemed to revolve around me, and to a lesser extent, my younger brother. Before I had time to ponder it, there was a knock on the door. I braced myself for my mother coming in to ask why I was taking so long.

"Yes?"

"Erica, it's me, Hayden. Your mother told me you were up here. I was hoping to have a word with you."

"Just coming," I replied with a sigh. I'd much rather speak to Hayden than my mother right now. She needed time to cool down, but it was just putting off the inevitable. Pulling myself out of the bath, I wrapped the towel Dora had left out for me around myself and padded to the door leaving wet footprints on the sparkly tiles. I opened the door a crack, aware that the only clothes I had in the bathroom was my drenched nightgown. Hayden raised his eyebrows at my lack of clothes, but I brushed past him, deciding I'd done enough blushing in one day to last a lifetime. Besides, it was only Hayden.

"Aren't you coming?" I asked when I realized he wasn't following me. He shook himself out of his daze and picked up his speed to match mine.

I cursed my mother for leaving me in the bathroom with nothing but a towel as I walked past some of the palace guards, trying to ignore their wide-eyed stares.

Thankfully, my bedroom wasn't that far, and as soon as the door closed behind me, I hopped into the walk-in wardrobe and pulled on a pair of jeans and a t-shirt.

"I think I preferred you in the towel," joked Hayden playfully as I came back into the bedroom. I threw the first thing I could find at him, which just happened to be a stuffed unicorn. How appropriate I should have toys of imaginary creatures in my room. With the way this day was turning out, I wouldn't be surprised if it turned into a real one.

Fortunately, it didn't. It just bounced of Hayden's head and landed on the floor.

"What's up?" I asked, sitting next to him on the bed.

"The wedding."

"Oh." What with everything else that had happened in the last twenty-four hours, I'd completely forgotten about it. I thought back to the conversation I'd had with my parents the day before. The last thing I'd said to them was that I'd think about it. Well, I'd thought about it, and there was no way I was going to go ahead with it. Not now. Having a husband with a ship would be nice, but it would be nothing compared to what I was going to have to give up. If I married Hayden, I wouldn't be able to see *him* again, the stranger.

I sighed. I was already due to have one argument with her today, now it seemed I could add another to the list. "Don't worry. It's not happening. I'll tell my mother later. She'll just have to cancel it all. It's her own fault for planning it without asking us. You'll still be able to date Astrid. I haven't seen her since the night of the party, but I assured her that there is nothing between us."

He cast his eyes downwards. I noticed he'd picked up a cushion from the bed and was now fiddling with the edge of it, a nervous habit I hadn't noticed before. Hayden was not known for being the nervous type.

"That's just it," he mumbled almost under his breath. I had to strain my ears to hear him. "Your parents have sent Astrid away. Some guards came to her house a couple of hours ago and took her."

I could barely believe it. "What? Why would they do that?"

His face adopted a look of intense sadness as he looked back up at me. I could almost feel his heart breaking just by his expression. I hadn't been exactly sure how it was between Hayden and Astrid, if it was just a fling or something more serious. But now, looking at him, I knew. He really loved her. "I guess because they don't want her getting in the way between us."

I screwed up my eyes in frustration. Hayden was my best friend, and I loved him. Not in the way he loved Astrid, but he meant the world to me. The two of us marrying would spoil everything. I knew for certain I didn't want to be his wife. Whether or not he decided to marry Astrid would have to be his own decision, not one given to him.

I took hold of his hand. He felt so different to the stranger. His skin was so much softer. Just thinking of the man who'd changed everything, the man whose name I still didn't know, made me sigh. This was all wrong.

"Where did she get taken?" I asked as softly as I could, hoping he knew the answer. I was pretty sure my parents wouldn't tell me if I asked them.

Hayden dropped the cushion and picked up the unicorn I'd thrown at him instead. I tried to ignore the fact he was absentmindedly unpicking the stitches on it. "Her mother told me she'd been taken to her aunt's house for the next two weeks."

"And where is that?" I asked, thinking I might have to make a visit.

"On the border of Eshen."

"Where exactly on the border?" I asked, knowing that I'd have to listen carefully if I was going to find the place.

"I don't know the address, but she told me it's a pink house in a town called Spirit, right on the very border. I know what you are thinking, and it's not going to happen. You won't be able to bring her back in time."

I sat up straight on the bed and took a deep breath. I hated being told what I could and couldn't do. I had been all my life, and it seemed it was happening a whole lot more frequently this past week. "Hayden Harrington-Blythe! I will go to her and bring her back. I'm eighteen now. My parents can't stop me from leaving the palace if I want to."

Hayden almost smiled, but the light in his eyes died. "I think you are wrong. There is no way you will get to leave the palace before the wedding, but that's not even the problem."

"So, what is the problem?"

He looked at me in such a way that had my heart falling. Something big was happening. I could see it in his eyes. I'd never in my whole life seen him look so desolate, so utterly distressed. When he did answer me, his voice was choked, almost as if he couldn't bear to get the words out

The wedding date has been moved up. Your mother called everyone this morning to tell them. We are due to marry in three days' time.

Away from it all

"What?" I stood up, outraged. "They said it would ultimately be my choice. I only spoke to them about this yesterday."

Hayden stood up and hugged me tightly, not because I was upset, but because I was shaking with anger. Like the good friend he was, he always knew how to calm me down. He knew me better than I knew myself. Oh, how I loved him then, but in the wrong way. It would have been so much easier if I loved him and he loved me in the right way, the way people should love each other.

Hayden stroked my hair as he spoke. "I guess something changed between then and now because an hour ago, one of the palace messengers came to the house and told my parents what would be happening. He said I was to be ready in three days. My mother called her friends and they confirmed that they had been called about the change of date. It's causing quite a panic. People are worried they won't find dresses in time."

I know he was joking to make me feel better, but it wasn't helping.

I pulled away from him. This was all because of what I'd done— because I'd gone out to sea. I'd betrayed my parents. I could understand them being angry with me, but to ruin my life and Hayden's because of it, well that was ridiculous. Something had changed within the last week. Something to prompt this stupid idea of Hayden and me. I just had to find out what it was before it was too late.

"Wait here," I demanded, stalking out of the room. The guard stationed along my corridor raised an eyebrow as I walked past him purposefully. I glared back at him, and he averted his eyes the way he was supposed to. Not that it was his fault, but he was part of it, this stupid, archaic system. At least, he was allowed to leave when his shift ended. I took the stairs to the bottom floor two at a time. Behind me, I could hear Hayden shouting me, having obviously ignored me telling him what to do.

My mother was knitting when I burst into her parlor. Knitting! She never knitted. I could tell it was a way to keep her hands busy while she talked to me. She'd known this was coming.

Despite her hands telling me she was nervous, she had a sly smile on her face, showing me that she'd won. I loved my mother, but at that point, I hated her too.

"What's this about me being married in three days?" I demanded.

"I see you've spoken with Hayden." As she said it, Hayden bounded in behind me.

"We aren't getting married," I said, my hands on my hips. "Neither of us wants to. We don't love each other in that way, and we are both eighteen. There is literally nothing you can say or do that will get me to walk down that aisle in three days' time."

"I'm guessing Hayden didn't tell you everything?" she replied. Her fingers moved furiously as she knitted, dropping stitches left and right.

I turned to look at Hayden, who was now standing beside me.

My mother continued, "If Hayden doesn't marry you in three days, his father will lose his position of Admiral of the Fleet. Along with his title, his house will be taken from him as will a considerable pension that was going to be given to him when he retires in five years."

I stood there, my mouth agape. What had happened to my wonderful mother that she would turn so ugly? There was no rhyme or reason to it. She'd always been strict but fair. Now she was a monster.

"I don't understand. Why do you want me to marry Hayden so badly? You've never even mentioned it before this past week." Tears of frustration began to pool at the corners of my eyes.

My mother dropped the knitting needles to her lap and looked me right in the eye. "I want you to marry Hayden, so you don't fall in love with anyone else. Someone who can only cause you pain."

She was talking about him, the stranger. Why did it even matter to her, and what did she mean about causing me pain. The only one hurting me right now was her.

I sucked in a deep breath between my teeth, trying to build up the confidence to tell her the truth.

"You know what?" I said as the tears streamed down my face. "It may be too late for that."

I turned, barging past Hayden who made no attempt to stop me and ran right through the entrance hall to the great hall. The tables and chairs had all been cleared away from my birthday party, but I could see boxes of wedding decorations piled up along the side.

"Stop her!" my mother yelled as I pelted through the hall. There were many ways to get to the sea from the palace, but the quickest route was via the great hall balcony.

I pushed the great doors open, aware that there were now numerous people after me. I didn't care. I'd gotten enough of a head start. I ran as fast as I could down the walkway to the lower level and to the promenade. The guard at the bottom, the same one who'd been there the night before, jumped right in front of me, blocking my way. Behind me, the other guards were catching up, and if I didn't think of something soon, I was going to get caught and dragged back to the palace. To my right, was the palace wall, but to my left, a railing. Without pausing, I ran to it and hopped right over the edge. It was much further down than I'd anticipated, and my ankle turned painfully as I hit the paving stones below.

Crossing the rocks was agony as each step with my right foot sent razor-sharp pains shooting up my leg. The guards were catching up, and behind them, I could hear both Hayden and my mother shouting my name. And still, I carried on, limping over the jagged rocks, splashing through the rock pools, not caring that my shoes were wet. I just knew I had to get away from them all. At the water's edge, I hesitated. Small waves broke, sending sea foam spraying over my legs. My right foot was swollen so badly it was threatening to break apart my shoe, and yet, I didn't care. With a quick look over my shoulder to see the guards almost upon me, I dove straight into the waves and began to sink below the water.

"Help me!" I shouted out in my mind, keeping my mouth clamped firmly shut. Without the stranger, the ocean was a much scarier place. My eyes stung with the salty water and I struggled not to panic as the seconds passed, each one bringing me closer to drowning. With the stranger, I'd been able to see. Now, everything looked murky. I tried swimming a little, hoping to move away from the rocks, but my arms didn't seem to want to cooperate.

Panic set in. What had I done? In my desperation to get away, I'd mistakenly thought the stranger would be there to save me as he had done before.

"Help me!" I repeated, trying to concentrate on an image of the stranger's face in my mind in the hope that would make him hear me better.

Behind me, I felt the water churn. I turned around swiftly to see someone had jumped into the water. It was Hayden. He'd jumped in to save me. Unlike my parents, his mother and father had sent him for swimming lessons from a very young age, and he was perfectly happy in the water.

He reached out, grabbed me around my waist and tried to pull me to the surface. The second my head went above water, I knew it would all be over. The guards would haul us both out, and we'd have to marry in three days. I wanted to articulate this to him, but I couldn't. I couldn't talk and speaking to him with my mind had no effect the way it did with the stranger. The only way I could escape this madness was for him to let me go. I squeezed his arm lightly, hoping he'd understand I didn't want to fight him. I was doing this for him as well as me, and then I raised my leg and kicked backward sharply with my left foot. Almost immediately, he let go. Using his body as leverage I pushed off against him with my good leg and drifted away from him.

"I'm so sorry," I said with my mind, knowing he wouldn't hear it.

Swiveling around in the water, I looked to see that he was okay. I'd hurt him, but hopefully, not enough to stop him being able to swim back to the surface. To my surprise, he'd gotten over the shock and was now swimming towards me, giving it another try to pull me to the surface. Why didn't he understand that bringing me back was essentially the end of him and Astrid?

My lungs were straining from keeping in the last bit of oxygen that I had, but I had to get away from him. I kicked my legs behind me, ignoring the pain shooting through my right foot.

He was a much better swimmer than me. I was barely swimming at all, just copying the motions I'd seen others do, but I was moving. I felt something brush against my leg and knew it was Hayden. This time, when he caught me, I knew I'd have to let him, because I was almost out of oxygen. Another few seconds and my brain would tell me to take a deep breath, and at that point, I'd inhale sea water. As Hayden's hand brushed my leg again, I felt a yank as I was pulled away from him at a high speed. I couldn't see anything, but I could finally breathe underwater again. It was him! I relaxed, letting him pull me through the ocean, past seaweed drifts and strange ocean creatures until we came to the same underwater cave he'd taken me to the day before. We both drifted up to the surface and took a deep breath at the same time. Before I had a chance to speak, his lips were on mine. Thoughts of Hayden and my mother flew right out of my head. I closed my eyes, relishing his touch, his tail wrapped around my body, his arms on my waist. Water dripped from his hair and mine down our faces. The kiss itself was salty as I'd come to expect from him, but unlike the temperature of the cave, his lips were warm and gentle.

"What were you saying sorry for?" he asked as he pulled apart from me. I thought back to earlier, trying to remember the last time I'd apologized.

"Oh, I was saying it to Hayden. He was trying to pull me to the surface to save me, and he wouldn't let me go. I hope he's ok."

The stranger furrowed his brow. *"Who's Hayden?"*

I swam as best I could to the little beach. It was much lighter now than it had been the last time I was here. I looked up to see a few more small holes in the ceiling where the sun filtered through. I scooted up to one of the warmer parts of the beach. As I pulled myself up onto the damp sand, my ankle gave another shot of pain. I groaned, and as I looked down, I could see it had swelled up and turned a horrible black-purple color that went right down to under the top of my shoe.

When the stranger saw it, he swam to me and took my ankle in his hand. I flinched before realizing it didn't hurt. Whatever he was doing to it, it was not painful. He ran his hands over the swelling and almost immediately heat spread through my leg, and the pain began to seep out. As I watched, my ankle turned from black to blue to red and back to the pale pink the rest of my leg was.

"How did you do that?" I asked, fascinated. I wiggled my foot, and it didn't hurt.

"Another part of my magic," he answered, taking my shoes off and placing them in the sand. He gave me a grin that melted my heart. *"Are you going to tell me who Hayden is, or do I have to guess?"*

"Why? Are you jealous?" I asked playfully, expecting him to say no.

"I'm jealous of any man right now," he answered simply. I wasn't quite sure I understood what he meant.

How could I describe Hayden? It was so complicated. He was everything to me, my friend, my brother, my partner in crime. "He's my best friend," I replied simply.

The stranger swam up to the beach and lay down beside me. His long hair dipped in the sand, and I had to resist the urge to run my fingers through it.

"Why were you trying to get away from him if he is your best friend? I heard you calling for help and thought someone was trying to hurt

you. It was only because I could see you were low on breath that I dragged you away rather than fought him."

"Hayden would never hurt me." I sighed and lay back on the beach. Beside me, I let the sand run through my fingers. A warm hand took mine.

"So, what happened?"

Turning my head to the left, I saw he had lain out next to me. His hair fanned out on the beach, and tiny yellow dots of sand were plastered to his wet skin.

I told him everything. How my mother had always had an unreasonable phobia of water and how it had gotten so much worse since my eighteenth birthday. I hesitated for a moment, unsure whether to tell him about the wedding to Hayden, but I knew there was no point keeping it back. He could read my mind.

When I was finished, he didn't say a word. Instead, he rested his head on his hand and looked at me. I could almost see his mind whirring, but he didn't seem upset.

"What is it?" I asked after he'd been silent for more than two minutes. I spoke with my mouth, but when he answered, it was with his mind.

"I've got an idea to help you out of this. I think I know how we can stop it...that is, if you want to."

Wedding planning

Of course, I wanted to. Not just for me but for Hayden and for Astrid too. Whatever was going on in my mother's head was all about me. I was convinced that it really had nothing to do with Hayden at all.

When the stranger told me the plan, I could barely believe the audacity of it and yet anything was better than the alternative.

I ran my fingers down his face. The plan meant that not only would Hayden and Astrid be happy, but I would be too. I looked at him, my stranger and wondered if the cost was too great.

His green eyes glistened in the shaft of light, and his hair looked almost blue. He was so strange and so beautiful, and yet, I didn't really know him. All we'd shared were a few snatched hours and a kiss here and there. I didn't even know his name. In all the time we'd spent together, I didn't know what he was called. More importantly, apart from that first time when he'd rescued me from the sinking ship, I'd not heard his voice. Not really. Since then, he'd communicated to me through his mind.

"What is your name?" I asked, winding a lock of his hair around my finger.

"Ari," he replied. *"Ari-El"*

"Ari," I repeated back. I'd never heard a name like it before in Trifork, but then he wasn't from Trifork. He was from another world entirely, a world that I wanted to explore.

I wanted to know more, to know everything about him, but more than that, I wanted to keep this feeling, to just be with him.

I inched my way down the beach, easing my way into the water of the underground lagoon. I loved how warm the water was and how I felt, moving my body effortlessly through it. I floated backward, my arms and legs spread out.

I closed my eyes, enjoying the sensation of floating and the thought that my problem was going to be solved. I knew I needed to get home to face the music, but I wasn't going to rush. I heard a splash, and then I was pulled under the water. Ari swam around me playfully. Now, that light filtered in through the ceiling, I could see the whole of the underwater world, a whole living ecosystem under the rocks. I watched as

Ari swam around me, showing off, and yet touching base with me every few seconds so I could breathe. He held my hand and swam me around letting me play with the fishes and try swimming by myself.

If Ari's plan panned out, I'd be able to spend as much time as I wanted getting to know this underwater world, and no one would be able to stop me.

He took me out to the open sea where we swam for miles. A pod of dolphins joined us, diving in and out of the water. The sun sparkled off the water's surface sending shimmers of light down into the depths. We swam so far out, I could barely see the coast anymore. All my troubles were back there. Out here, I was as free as I wanted to be. Out here, I could do what I wanted as long as Ari was beside me. Out here, I was happy.

It was the perfect day, or it was until the sound of the water being chopped up on the surface spoiled the tranquility.

"What's that?" I asked in alarm, looking up to where black shapes blocked out the sun.

Ari had seen them too. He pulled me quickly downwards to the seabed as more light was blocked out.

He put his arm around me protectively, his face set in a grimace. *"It's ships, boats. It's your people. They are looking for you."*

I knew that my parents would want to find me, but I was surprised at the lengths they were going to, to do it. There were so many boats above us, I could barely make out the gaps of sky between them. As I watched, a diver jumped into the water with a splash, quickly followed by two more. Everywhere I looked, people in diving gear were hurling themselves from the boats.

"We need to get out of here," I blurted, trying to swim away from the people. They were everywhere now, hundreds of them.

Ari didn't answer, he didn't have to. Instead, he pulled me through the water quickly, keeping to the depths in the hope that we wouldn't be seen.

"Where are we going?" I asked as the water barraged past, leaving me almost blind with the speed we were going.

He stopped for a second and faced me. I could see him clearly now that we were away from the boats.

"I have to ask you something, and I'd like you to be honest with me."

I nodded, fearful of what he would ask me.

"When I first met you on that beach, I knew instantly that you were someone special. When you asked me to kiss you after I gave you CPR, I wanted to. I also knew that you were someone special to other people. The fact that so many people were out looking for you told me that. I don't know much about the land dwellers, but I knew enough to know that the people searching for you were palace guards. I recognized their uniforms. When I left you, I couldn't get you out of my mind."

"I felt the same way about you," I interrupted. He smiled at me and then continued.

"I spent hours watching the palace, trying to figure out a way to meet you that wouldn't terrify you. It was then I saw that there was to be a ball for your birthday. I came onto the land, stole a suit, and after putting it into a waterproof bag, I swam around to the back of the palace and sneaked in. Maybe I was hoping to get you out of my system. I don't even know.

"When I saw you in that dress and saw you blush when you saw me, I knew you felt the same way I did. Dancing with you was the singularly most exciting thing I'd ever done. No, scrap that. Kissing you afterward was the most exciting thing. If I'd gone to the ball to get you out of my mind, I'd completely failed. I knew I wanted to spend more time with you. I guess I knew earlier because I'd already written that

note and left it in my pocket, hoping you'd find it."

My heart was thumping madly with the things he was telling me. I wanted to tell him that he excited me more than he could ever know, but I knew I should let him finish what he had to say. I wanted to listen to his words. They echoed my own feelings so completely.

"It took you so long to find it that I thought that I'd made a mistake and gotten it wrong. I was so happy when you came to me. Of course, by then I knew you were a princess. The heir to the Throne of Trifork, no less."

"Yes, so?"

"So, that makes our relationship difficult."

"I don't see how," I replied although that was a lie. The hundred or so boats we'd left behind told me that much.

"I just want to know if this is worth it for you. We barely know each other. Being with me is going to make your life so complicated. Mine too in ways I didn't think about when I went to your palace that night. I've been ignoring it for days, too caught up in just being with you, but as you can see, it's caught up with us."

"What are you asking me?" My heart was threatening to thump right out of my chest. I

never felt cold in the water with him, but a chill was running through me now.

"I'm asking if you really want to do this...to be with me. I could easily take you back to the boats. They'll pull you up, and you'll go back to living the life you were supposed to."

I didn't even need to think about it. *"This is the life I'm supposed to lead. Here with you. I can feel it. It's not even just you. There's something about the ocean. I feel like I belong here."*

His expression changed then. The serious face he'd had when talking to me softened, and I could see the relief in it. He wanted me, and I wanted him, and for that moment in time, that's all I cared about.

"In that case, we need to get you away from here. For now, at least."

"I will have to go back at some point soon if we are going to put that plan of yours into action," I reminded him.

"Soon," he replied, *"but not just yet!"*

Ari took my hand, both of us knowing that our plan, our decision would change the course of the history of Trifork, and to be perfectly honest, I didn't care. Trifork would carry on as always, and in a few years, no one would remember the royal wedding. At least, I hoped not.

We swam through the water, leaving the boats behind us. Well, Ari was swimming. I was doing my best to kick my legs, so he wasn't doing all the work.

Ahead of us, rising up from the ocean floor, a great underwater city loomed. I hadn't put much thought into where Ari lived before now. I guess I was expecting some kind of underwater utopia where beautiful mermaids sat on coral beds, brushing their hair. What I didn't expect was a real city. A place with streets and buildings and people going about their business in much the same way as the people in Trifork did. Huge living monoliths of coral, mud, and bits of flotsam and jetsam from passing ships came together to create buildings, real buildings with windows and doors. Sea flowers bloomed everywhere, on the streets and on the sides of buildings, painting the whole town a riot of living color. Schools of prettily colored fish swam in and out of the buildings, and sea creatures scurried along the floor. To top it all off, sun glinted off the buildings making the whole place sparkle. It was as if the whole place was its very own ecosystem, which I guess in fact it was.

"It's beautiful," I whispered in my head, in awe of the spectacle before us.

"It's Havfrue. It's my home," replied Ari simply.

We swam through avenues of salmon pink coral as other merpeople went about their business. The few that did catch sight of us together either dashed away nervously or gave us disapproving looks as we passed. Just like I hadn't really thought much about the town, I'd not really put much thought into the other merfolk either. Unlike above land where most people were either dark-haired or blonde, down here the merpeople's hair was every color of the rainbow. I'd never thought how rare my mother's and my red hair was before, but now, seeing this, I realized that the shade of red both our hair shared would not look out of place here at all. I'd never actually met anyone before now with quite the same shade of red—not ginger, not strawberry blond, but flaming red hair. Here in Havfrue, I spotted a number of people with the very same shade. In the distance, loomed a building or a series of buildings, it was hard to tell which; but it was huge, towering over the whole city.

"What's that?" I asked, pointing to the monolith in the distance.

"That's where the king lives. I'm not going to take you there. The king would not be happy to know there was a land dweller here in Havfrue. He believes land dwellers to be our mortal enemy."

I must have looked nervous because he added *"He won't find out if we keep to the outskirts. Here we are."*

In front of us, was a small building made out of the most beautiful blue-purple coral. Small orange and black fish darted in and out of the entrance. Inside, was a small room with no furniture. Light poured in from the window illuminating the dramatic colors of the place. Apart from a few shells on the sandy bed, the whole place was empty. Ok, not quite empty, in the corner, was a small octopus.

Ollie! I opened my mouth in surprise and got a mouthful of water. I needed to remember not to do that again. The small creature swam over to me and swam over my fingers.

We spent the morning playing with Ollie, hidden away from the world in Ari's small room. I wanted to stay there forever. If I had any choice in the matter at all, I might very well have, but I knew I'd have to go back to the shore to face the music sooner rather than later. Ari's plan wouldn't work if we lazed around all day in the water, no matter how much I wanted it to. When the sun was high in the sky, I decided it was time to go back.

As we swam closer to the shore, I could see the sheer amount of guards out combing the seafront, waiting for us. Hundreds of small sailing boats bobbed around on the water by the coast waiting for me to come home.

"You can't come back to the shore with me," I said, using my mind to communicate with Ari.

"How are you going to get back without me? You can't swim remember?"

"I can," I insisted, tugging my hand from his. After attempting a couple of strokes and barely keeping my head above water, I had to admit it was a lost cause. I'd drown long before I got near the coast. As I cast my eyes along the line of small boats, I spotted one I recognized. With a yellow stripe around it, I knew it belonged to Hayden. So, he was out looking for me too.

"That's Hayden's boat," I said, this time speaking aloud. I pointed to the boat with the yellow stripe. "If you can get me to him, you should be able to swim away with no problem. Hayden won't hurt you when I tell him who you are."

The yellow striped boat was not the closest, nor was it far from the other boats which would make things harder, but with Ari pulling me along underwater, we were able to get to it undetected. I reached up and grabbed the edge, keeping the rest of me underwater so I wouldn't be seen.

"Go!" I said in my mind. *"I'll stay underwater as long as I can so you can get away."*

141

He kissed me briefly then turned, swishing his tail behind him and churning up the water. When I could hold my breath no longer, I pulled myself up to the surface and gulped in great breaths of air.

"Hayden!" I shouted up to him, but it wasn't Hayden's head that appeared over the side of the boat. It was my mother's.

A huge pair of hands came over the side, and I realized they belonged to my father. They must have known I'd go for Hayden's boat. A man I didn't recognize sailed the boat, and Hayden was nowhere to be seen.

"Where's Hayden?" I asked defiantly as my father hauled me over the side.

My mother's face was contorted in fury, but there was something else there too. She was genuinely scared. I glared at her, expecting her to shout at me; but instead, she moved towards me, bringing me into a hug. Her body shook with sobs as she held me close to her. What was going on? One minute she was angry, the next she was fearful. I looked to my father who remained stoic, keeping his eyes on the coast. He gave the command, and the captain turned the small boat around and headed for land. As I looked around me, the other boats followed.

"Promise me you'll not run away again," my mother said, tears in her eyes. "Promise me you'll have the wedding to Hayden. He's been so worried about you. He thought you might drown."

I nodded my head, completely confused by what was happening. It was a promise I only half intended to keep.

That night during dinner, when I'd bathed and dressed, my mother informed me that Hayden was now under house arrest. Even though he'd tried to stop me from leaving and had absolutely no idea about Ari, my mother didn't want him running away any more than she wanted me to. Because of this, both us were confined to our rooms in our respective houses for the next three days. Knowing what I knew, being stuck in my room didn't bother me. I spent the next three days being the perfect, obedient daughter and princess. By day, I attended dress fittings, tried cakes, and watched the palace staff decorate the great hall where not only the reception was due to take place, but the wedding too.

I offered my opinion of bridesmaid dress colors even though I didn't really have anyone I cared about enough to be a bridesmaid. If Astrid was still around, I'd have chosen her. But as she wasn't, I had to make do with my two younger cousins who lived at the other side of the kingdom and whom I barely knew.

Nighttime was another matter. I spent endless hours sitting on my balcony, gazing out to sea, watching the moonlight shimmer over calm waves. In all the time I spent out there, I didn't see Ari, and for three days, I couldn't communicate with him. However much I tried speaking to him through my mind, he never replied.

The day of the wedding arrived all too soon. My mother woke me early with a cup of coffee and a breezy smile on her face.

"Good morning, good morning," she trilled as she flung back the curtains. I doubted she'd feel the same when the day was over. I took the mug from her gratefully and took a deep gulp, enjoying the caffeine hit as it went down.

"Get yourself in the bath quickly," she said, ushering me out of bed as I gripped the mug handle tightly so as not to spill the coffee on the bed.

I headed out onto the balcony as my mother turned the taps on in the small en-suite bathroom. The day was shaping up to be beautiful, the weather perfect for a royal wedding. A single, white cloud flittered across an otherwise perfect, blue sky, and the sun warmed my cheeks.

"Your bath is nearly ready," my mother yelled from my bedroom. "I'll send someone up with your dress."

I thanked her, praying she'd leave me alone. This was going to be one of the most important days of my life, and I wanted to enjoy it...or get through it in peace.

As my balcony looked over the ocean behind the palace, I had no idea just how many people had turned up to see me. I was pretty sheltered here, although I could see a number of boats out on the sea, no doubt with journalists and photographers trying to be the first to get a photo of me in my wedding dress. Well, they weren't in luck. Having just gotten out of bed, I was currently wearing a t-shirt and some pajama bottoms that had seen better days. That might have been newsworthy in itself, but from the sea, my bottoms would be hidden by the balcony railings. I downed my coffee with a sigh, waved at the people on the boats and headed inside to my future, whatever that was going to be.

I washed my hair thoroughly and towel dried it, knowing that my mother had hired a professional to style it. Wrapping the towel around my waist, I headed to the bedroom, wondering what exactly I'd find there. I'd been measured for the dress, but with so little time to have a dress fitting, I'd not actually seen the finished thing. Had this been a wedding I really cared about, I might have been upset that I'd not chosen my own dress, but as it was, my biggest concern was whether it fit and how quickly I could run in it.

On the bed, was a dress cover with a coat hanger at the top. I knew my mother had style, she was famous for her dress sense, so I knew whatever I found in there would be pretty spectacular. I unzipped it and pulled out a beautiful white dress. It had a love heart neckline and nipped in at the waist before billowing out in a skirt of the slightest hint of pink. On top of that, delicate lace flowers cascaded down the entire length of it. It was not what I would choose for myself, but I couldn't deny that it was beautiful.

If I wasn't already a princess, I'd certainly feel like one in it. Next to the dress was some beautiful white underwear. A white corset, much sexier than anything I'd ever worn before, and some pretty lace panties to match sat beside some stockings and a pair of the most beautiful, sparkling shoes. It was almost a pity I wouldn't be wearing them. Instead, I dug a white strapless bra and pants from my drawer and put them on before easing the dress over my head. I hid the bridal underwear and gorgeous shoes under my bed and fished out a pair of running shoes, thanking my mother's sense of propriety for giving me a dress that was long enough to cover them.

Looking in the mirror, I saw a beautiful princess on the morning of her wedding day. If only I didn't feel like a traitor who was just about to break her mother's heart.

"Are you ready?" My mother shouted from outside my bedroom door. I took one last look at myself in the mirror. I was as ready as I'd ever be.

The wedding

My mother hovered around as the make-up artist and hairdresser worked their magic on me. It all felt like such a waste, knowing that no one was really going to see any of it. My hair was weaved into a set of beautiful braids which were then covered over with a white veil, customary of any bride in Trifork. It was this that was going to allow me to pull off the stunt that I knew would shock everyone in Trifork and possibly give my own mother a heart attack in the process.

"You look beautiful." My mother beamed with pride as the veil was lowered over my face. My heart lurched knowing how badly I was about to let her down. Tears streamed down her face, tears of happiness, which made me feel terrible at what I was about to do to her. She'd been acting awfully in the past few weeks, but it was out of character for her. Still, this wasn't about getting her back or some misguided attempt at revenge. It was stopping something that I knew in my heart to be wrong.

I lifted my hand and wiped my mother's cheek. "I love you," I said, wishing it didn't have to be this way. I waited as the make-up artist touched up my mother's face and then stood ready to head out to the great hall. My mother linked her arm in mine and walked me out into the corridor. Already I could hear the guests seating themselves in the thousands of chairs that had been laid out for the occasion. Later, the chairs would be rearranged around tables for a feast that was currently being prepared in the kitchens below us.

I pictured Hayden standing at the front of the great hall waiting for me. He knew nothing that was about to happen, and for that, I was glad. I didn't want him getting in trouble. He would be standing up there, dressed in his best clothing, waiting for a ceremony that would bind us together forever—or so, he thought. Outside the palace, the screams and cheers of the public and media were so loud that I could hear them through the thick outer walls of the palace. At the double doors to the great hall, my mother handed me over to my father, who was due to walk me down the aisle. He cut a dashing figure in his white suit and purple sash. My mother gave me a wink as she slipped between the double doors, careful not to open them too wide lest someone see me before they should. Behind me, my two little cousins stood side by side, a picture of cuteness in their matching purple dresses, flowers in their hair.

"Are you ready?" my father asked, a look of unhappiness on his face. I realized then that this was not his doing. Despite being the supreme ruler of Trifork, he had no say in today's proceedings. This was all my mother. Not for the first time, I wondered what was going on with her, but I didn't have too much time to ponder it. I had to put the plan into action first.

"I need the bathroom!" I lied, unlinking myself from my father's arm.

"Just be quick. They are waiting for you," huffed my father. I shot him a wink and disappeared into the small bathroom reserved for guests. Like any bathroom in a public place, it was actually a set of stalls with a mirror running along the length of it with basins in front.

One of my grandmother's friends was in there, touching up her lipstick. She seemed surprised to see me in there with her.

"The wedding is nearly starting. You should go and find your place," I coaxed. She gave me a hurried nod and left.

"Astrid?" I called quietly, bending down to look under the stall doors. Slowly one of the stalls opened and there stood my friend looking utterly radiant with her golden hair cascading in curls around her shoulder.

"You look amazing," I said, quickly.

"You look beautiful," she spoke at the same time. We both began to laugh. With little time afforded to me, I pulled the wedding dress quickly over my head. Astrid stepped into it. As she was slightly bigger around the bust than me, she had to squeeze into it. Once she was finished, I took off the veil and placed it on her head, tucking the blonde curls behind her ears.

"Remember, Hayden is going to expect me under there. I don't know what will happen, but with any luck, the wedding will be over when he lifts the veil and sees who he married."

"Do you think he really wants to marry me?" she asked uncertainly.

I shook my head as I pulled on the t-shirt and jeans she'd brought for me to wear. "I honestly don't know, but I do know that given the choice, he'd rather marry you than me. If the two of you decide that you want to stay married, you can have a much more intimate wedding further down the line. A renewal of vows, so to speak."

Astrid gave me a shy smile. "I just don't want to marry someone who doesn't know who he's marrying. It's so sneaky."

I gave her a hug. "I'm so grateful to you for doing this. If you really don't want to marry Hayden this way, pull the veil up before the end of the ceremony. I only need about ten minute's head start. I'm meeting Ari down by the rocks. Tell my family I'll be home in a few weeks once the shock has worn off and tell them I'm sorry."

"That Ari is bloody gorgeous," she mused, giving herself a quick glance in the mirror. "I can quite understand now why you don't want to get married."

"You are bloody gorgeous," I told her, and I meant it. Hayden was one lucky man. He was also in for one hell of a shock.

When she walked from the bathroom dressed as me, I waited five minutes. Just enough time for everyone to be paying attention to the bride.

As quickly as I could, I climbed out through the small window and dropped to the ground, landing in one of the palace garden's flower beds. There were more guards than usual, owing to the nature of the day, plus I had to worry about the sheer numbers of media people milling around. I'd plotted my route carefully over the course of the last few days, but there was still every chance I'd be spotted.

Astrid had left me a cap and sunglasses. It wasn't much in the way of a disguise, but as everyone could see *me* walking down the aisle on big screens that had been erected around the palace, it was better than nothing. Going straight down to the rocks was impossible. I already knew how many guards were down there fending off the hordes of media. The only way out was to go to the front entrance of the palace and mingle with the crowds. It was risky. Any number of things could go wrong, and it was very possible I'd be recognized. But it was the only way I could think of to get to the meeting place we'd set up. I had to time it exactly. The short run from the bathroom window at the side of the palace to the wall at the edge of the gardens had to be done at the precise moment that Astrid was walking down the aisle. Before that, and the guards were more likely to think it was me that was escaping. It wouldn't surprise me if my mother had put them on full alert for this to be a possibility. If I left it too late, Astrid might have already decided to lift her veil and the second she did that, the shorefront would be swamped with people looking for me. I'd picked this window because it was at the quietest side of the palace. A well-placed ladder enabled me to be able to be over the wall before I was caught and from there, I was in the outside world. I ended up in a street filled with onlookers. Thankfully, they were all facing one of the huge screens, and I was able to slip amongst them unnoticed. The streets were packed solid with people, most of whom were waving the flag of Trifork. There was so much excitement in the air for my wedding—if only I felt the same way. It seemed that the only two people in the whole kingdom who didn't want to see Hayden and I get married were Hayden and I.

The crowds were difficult to slip through. People were standing shoulder to shoulder and to push through them would get me noticed. Instead, I slipped up a side street away from the throng and in the opposite direction from where I needed to be. It was a much longer route, but I hoped with the streets being empty here, I'd get there both quicker and less likely to be noticed.

Two streets away from the palace and it was almost as if I'd gone into another world. All the shops were closed for the royal wedding and photos of Hayden and I filled all the storefronts. Before now, it hadn't occurred to me just how much of a big deal this was. Worry crept over me that I was doing the wrong thing. It had seemed so right when I was under the ocean discussing it with Ari, but now, in the cold light of day, standing all alone in the quietest market street in the whole kingdom, I was beginning to realize what a mistake it was. Taking a deep breath, I forced myself onward, giving myself a pep talk as I picked up the pace.

"It isn't a mistake," I mumbled under my breath. "I couldn't have married Hayden."

I wondered how he was feeling right now. Nervous, probably. The wedding was being televised all over the kingdom and most of the other kingdoms too, I was willing to bet. Would he be a little bit excited or would he be heartbroken knowing that Astrid would never be his? I hoped he wouldn't be angry with me when he found out who exactly was under that veil. I knew he was serious about Astrid, but they were both so young and hadn't been going out that long. Maybe Hayden's concerns weren't just that he had to marry me, but that he was forced to get married at all.

I gave a sigh at the mess I found myself in. In the distance, I could hear a flock of seagulls, reminding me where I was going. The call of the ocean was strong as if I'd always known I'd be a part of it someday. Of course, I'd always thought I wanted to sail above the sea but being below it was so much better than anything I'd ever dreamed.

The sea was in sight now. All I had to do was run and meet Ari. From there, I'd spend a few weeks with him, just enough time to let this whole wedding thing blow over, and I'd come home and apologize profusely.

I jogged until I hit the boardwalk. To my right, thousands of people surrounded the palace, but to my left, the beach was empty, exactly as Ari and I had planned. On the far left of the beach, before it turned into the sheer white cliffs that this part of the kingdom was famous for, were rocks similar to the ones behind the palace. It was at this point where Ari had arranged to meet me. With a sense of trepidation, I stepped out onto the beach. Before I took another step, I pulled my sneakers and socks off and let myself feel the sand between my toes. Because of my mother's crazy phobia about the ocean, I'd only ever been on a beach once, and that was because my new nanny at the time hadn't been told otherwise. She was fired the very next day. I was about four years old at the time, and Anthony was barely crawling, but I still remember how it felt to squash my feet into the warm sand. However much I wanted to, I couldn't stand around all day, playing on the beach. I needed to get to Ari before the wedding came to a standstill. Even as I thought it, a collective gasp had me turning my head. On the large screen at the far end of the beach near the walls of the palace, I saw Astrid's face. Seconds later, the picture dissolved into one of Hayden looking shell-shocked.

My time had run out, I needed to get to the sea now. Leaving my sneakers behind, I pelted through the sand until I came to the rocky outcrop. I couldn't see Ari, but I knew he was there. Walking out to the farthest point, I looked down into the water. Even though it was a beautiful day and the waves on the beach wouldn't knock over a toddler, here, they made me nervous.

"It's fine!" I breathed to myself, closing my eyes. I could breathe underwater when I was with Ari, so it wasn't like I was going to drown. Still, I'd have felt much more comfortable if I could have seen him under the water.

"Are you there?" I asked with my mind, hoping that my thoughts would travel through the air and the water. There was no answer. I tried again, this time shouting. My voice attracted a couple of guards at the far end of the beach. They were already out looking for me. It hadn't taken long at all!

Closing my eyes and taking a deep breath, I leapt as far as I could out into the foaming sea.

Almost immediately, the current took me and began to pull me out. I struggled to keep my head above water, waiting for those strong arms of Ari's to pull me down to the depths with him. As the waves crashed overhead and with a sinking heart, I realized he hadn't come, I was quite literally out of my depth, and I still couldn't swim.

Dark Water

The pull of the sea was strong, much stronger than I was used to. Had I not been drowning, I might have wondered why I was being swept along so quickly. The beach was a popular destination, and I'd spent many a day watching families playing there, skipping over the small waves. Even children as young as toddlers were often found dipping their toes in, so why had it suddenly become so dangerous? Below me, I could feel the sand, although here, it was covered in seaweed which made the experience so much more terrifying. With each step, I had to push up from the bottom to get my head above water so I could get a gasp of breath before going back under. At the same time, I had to fight off the fear that the seaweed was actually some gross creature.

Every time my head went above water, I could see I'd moved further and further along the beach. Without even trying, I was heading back towards the palace. There were so many people out on the beach now, no doubt looking for me, that I knew I would be rescued if I could keep coming up for breath the way I was doing. It was little consolation. Ok, I'd survive which was good, but my mother was going to have a field day with this. This was the third time in as many weeks that I'd nearly drowned. I was beginning to think she had a point about the sea being dangerous.

All around me, the water was dark, much more so than when I'd come out here with Ari. There was something weird going on, and I was right in the middle of it. Below the waterline, it was pitch black, despite it being a fine sunny day. On the brief snatches of time I was above water, I could see that the blackness only extended about fifty feet in every direction and I was directly in the center. Whatever this was, it was not a natural phenomenon. Something was causing this to happen.

My lungs strained with the effort of trying to keep above water and holding my breath, and my heart was pounding so hard it was painful.

I'd almost completely given up when someone grabbed me. For the briefest of seconds, I thought that Ari had finally come, but then I realized I was actually being pulled upwards not down. The water clung to me as I was hoisted over the side of a small boat with an outboard motor behind it. As soon as I was fully in the boat, the motor was put on full power, and we zoomed through the waves towards a small jetty by the palace.

The strange blackness receded after I was no longer in the water. I'd not seen it at all before I'd jumped in. It just kind of appeared from nowhere, pulling me away from the beach, and now it was disappearing as quickly as it had come. It reminded me of the time just before the *Erica Rose* went down. Just like today, that day had been calm and serene before the water turned black. This time, I'd been pulled out and to shore before the ocean had turned too turbulent.

One of the two men in the boat handed me a towel. Both men were palace guards. I didn't know either of them, but I could tell by their uniform.

I shivered as I took in the sight of the seafront. All the people that had come to see the royal wedding were now lining up watching me coming back to shore. Hundreds of cameras pointed at me, and I could see my cold, wet, miserable face projected onto one of the large screens where minutes before, the royal wedding had been showing. Right up to the boundary between the palace grounds and the public walkway, people were cheering the safe return of the princess. They'd come for one show and all gotten more than they had bargained for. This was turning out to be quite a spectacle for the masses. On the palace side, things were a different matter completely. A number of guards waited by the dockside to help me out, all with somber faces. I searched the line of people for my mother's face, but she wasn't there. My father was also absent. Maybe they were clearing up the mess on the inside, trying to explain to the guests why Astrid had taken my place.

Fear of what I would find when I got to the palace filled me. My parents would surely be angry with me. Maybe Hayden would be too. All the guests, many of which who had traveled a long way to see the royal princess wed, would no doubt have something to say about all of this too. I'd single-handedly messed everything up. Relations between our kingdom and the other eight would now be strained, not to mention my parents' relationship with the Harrington-Blythes. I didn't want to think about my relationship with anyone.

As I stepped up onto the jetty, I remembered that I'd not done this single-handedly at all. It hadn't even been my idea. I glanced back at the sea, now peaceful and without any trace of the sudden blackness that had engulfed me. Ari was out there somewhere. Why hadn't he come for me?

All eyes were upon me as I made my way through the palace, flanked by two guards. I didn't need to hear their thoughts to know what they were thinking.

Keeping my eyes firmly on the ground in front of me as I walked full of shame, barefoot, and dripping wet. Could this day get any worse?

Of course, it could. I still had my parents to deal with. My father would be angry, but my mother...well, it didn't bear thinking about.

My stomach churned more and more with each step closer to the great hall where it looked like I was being taken. All thoughts of being able to do this privately went out the window as the great hall doors were opened and I was faced with the fallout of my actions.

Most of the guests had already been escorted out, but there in the hall, looking at me in a way that made me feel even worse, were Hayden, Astrid, Hayden's parents, Anthony, and my father. My mother, the one person I was the most worried about, was nowhere to be seen.

I steeled myself for one hell of a talking to when I heard my mother's cries from behind me. I turned just as she launched herself at me.

"Oh, thank goodness, you are alright."

I put my arms around her as she sobbed into my shoulder. Judging by the expressions on the faces of all those around me, they were just as confused as I was.

"Erica," my father began, taking a step toward me. "Your actions have..."

"Stop!" my mother yelled, holding her hand out toward him, palm facing him. "Don't. Can't you see she's been through enough already? I'm taking her up to my room so I can look after her. You can sort this out down here, can't you?"

My father was behind me now as my mother was still hugging me and speaking to him over my shoulder, but I could well imagine the expression on his face. I'm pretty sure it echoed my expression of complete bewilderment.

"What about the wedding?" asked someone. It was Lord Harrington-Blythe.

My mother pulled herself back from me and faced him. Her lips pulled back tightly. "Can't you see my daughter is under enough stress? I don't care about the wedding. Do what you will."

With that, she took my hand and led me away from everyone up to her top-floor bedroom.

Despite the way in which she spoke to everyone else, I was still expecting a huge telling off as soon as we got to her room. It was her idea to have this wedding, after all. It was she that planned every little detail, and it was she who had insisted that I take part in it.

"I'm sorry," she said, sitting on the bed. "I'm so, so sorry."

She handed me a dress of hers to put on. I pulled off my wet clothes and eased myself into her dress. It was slightly too long for me, and I'm sure my hair dripping all over it was damaging the delicate fabric, but my mother didn't seem to notice or care, so neither did I.

I sat down beside her and placed my hand on her shoulder in an attempt to comfort her. This whole thing was baffling me, but I knew to rush her wouldn't work. I was just happy that I didn't seem to be in any kind of trouble.

"I thought...I thought..." she sniffed, the tears rolling freely down her face. I got up and grabbed a tissue from her nightstand before returning and handing it to her. I'd never seen her lose her composure like this. I couldn't even remember a time when she'd apologized for anything, whatever she was saying sorry for, would have to be huge to get her worked up into such a state.

"I'm sorry too," I offered for the want of anything else to say. It felt like I should be the one apologizing after all. This just started her on a fresh round of tears. She drew me into a hug, almost squeezing the life out of me. I wondered if this was all a ploy, and she was indeed trying to murder me by constricting my airway, but she let go and sat back, allowing me to breathe freely again.

She squeezed her eyes shut and took in a deep breath. It took her almost a minute to compose herself and steel herself to talk to me. "I have something to tell you. Something that I hoped I'd never have to share with anyone. It was so long ago, I'd almost convinced myself that it never happened, that it was some kind of dream, but then..."

Her voice trailed off as though she was remembering some long-forgotten memory.

"Why don't you start at the beginning?" I encouraged kindly. She was making no sense as it was.

She nodded her head slightly and mopped up the tears with an embroidered handkerchief she'd pulled from a pocket. The tissue I'd passed her lay unused but crumpled on the bed.

"I really didn't want to tell you this. You, of all people..."

"Please tell me," I urged. If she didn't begin to talk soon, I was afraid she'd begin crying again.

"A long time ago, around about the time I was your age, I didn't live here in Trifork. I lived somewhere very different indeed."

This was new information. I'd always been under the impression that my mother had been born here. I had no grandparents on her side, and she'd always led me to believe that she was an orphan down on her luck when she met my father at eighteen, and they'd fallen in love. It was a story of forbidden love as she was a commoner. I'd always found it so romantic. Echoes of my own romance with Ari popped into my head. Ever since I'd first met him, I'd had this thought that we'd end up like my own mother and father. Of course, now, I wasn't sure. I barely knew the guy and now, I realized all these thoughts I'd been having were simply silly teenage dreams. I tried to smother the crushing disappointment and focus on what my mother was trying to tell me.

"Where do you come from then?" I asked her, deliberately keeping my voice low so as not to upset her further. It felt like I was trying to encourage a scared bunny rabbit. This was *so* not the mother I knew.

She could barely look me in the eye as she spoke. I knew that whatever she was about to say was difficult for her. She took a deep breath and began to speak again.

"I was a woman of the ocean when I met your father."

I furrowed my brow in confusion. A woman of the ocean? What exactly did that mean? And then it dawned on me.

"Are you trying to tell me that you are a mermaid?"

As she looked up, I saw something in her eyes I'd never seen before but was completely familiar with. I'd seen the flecks of purple in Ari's eyes.

"Yes," she replied simply. "Yes, I am."

A secret uncovered

I gaped at my mother open-mouthed. "Does Daddy know?"

"No," she answered, shaking her head, "and I don't want him to know. He thinks I'm from Trifork just like you did. I told him the same story I've always told you, told everyone."

The whole thing was ridiculous, but I could see in her eyes it was true. It still didn't explain why she'd wanted me to marry Hayden or why she was so scared of the ocean. As a mermaid, or former mermaid, she should love the water.

"So, what happened?" I cajoled. "You said this started when you were about my age."

She nodded. "I was happily living out at sea, keeping away from the land dwellers. We keep to ourselves. Most people think we are imaginary, so few land dwellers have seen us. We knew how to keep away. Our greatest law was to never speak to those with legs. It was an easy law to keep as I never saw anyone with legs until one day I was swimming away from the town when I saw a man in the water. He was so strange to me. I didn't know it at the time, but he was a recreational deep-sea diver. I guessed he was looking for coral or oysters. I didn't know which. He was wearing a black wetsuit and goggles. On his back, he wore oxygen canisters. As I'd never seen a human before, I thought the wetsuit was his skin, and the goggles were his eyes. At first, I was terrified, but after a while, I became fascinated. The way he swam with flippers. He was, quite frankly, the strangest creature I'd ever laid my eyes on."

I tried to picture a deep-sea diver. For a woman who had never seen clothes before, I could quite well imagine how strange he would look to her.

"Every day I'd go to the same spot, and every day there was someone else diving. I guess a tour company took tourists out. One day, I decided to follow the boat to see where it went. It was foolish, and I knew at the time, I'd be in so much trouble from my parents, but the compulsion to find out about the land dwellers was too much."

"I guess disobeying one's parents runs in the family," I butted in. She gave me a wan smile and carried on.

"The boat came back here to the public jetty. I swam along the seafront until I saw a completely different type of land dweller. In reality, he was just wearing normal clothes, but I didn't know that then. He was out in the garden, just walking around mumbling to himself. I fell in love with him instantly. He was so handsome and looked so worried about something. I hid behind some rocks, desperately wanting to go up and speak to him, but I couldn't. I had a tail. There was no way I'd be able to get across all the rocks without legs, and if I did, I was afraid I'd scare him. So, I did something so terrible, something so stupid that to this day, I regret it with all my heart. I went to the sea witch."

"The sea witch?" An image of a green hag flying around underwater on a broom sprang to mind. A witch was another creature I'd thought was imaginary before this last couple of weeks. Nothing surprised me anymore. I was willing to bet if a leprechaun riding a pink unicorn strolled into the bedroom, I'd not batter an eyelid.

"She was...is the sea's most ferocious woman. She is the equivalent of the mayor up here and has some serious clout. Most of the merpeople are terrified of her. I was terrified of her, but I wanted to meet your father so badly that I mustered up the courage and sought her out.

"She told me she would give me legs on two conditions. One, that I would never be able to return to the ocean. My tail would be permanently gone, and two, that she would steal my voice."

I tried to wrap my head around what she was telling me.

"But you have a voice," I pointed out.

She hung her head again. "I thought that I would need my voice to talk to your father. How else would I get to know him if I couldn't talk to him?"

I thought back to all the times I'd *spoken* with Ari. The only time I remembered him using his audible voice was the first time we met when he saved me. I hadn't thought about it before now, but I wondered if he'd made a similar exchange with the sea witch. I'd seen him with legs after all. Unlike my mother, he kept his tail too. He was able to be one way in water and another on land.

"So, what did you offer?" I asked. The look on her face was enough to tell me that it was something terrible. Her eyes, already brimming with tears, began to overflow.

"I offered my firstborn child. At the time, I was so young that thoughts of children were so far away in the distance. I wasn't even sure I'd have children. It seemed like a good exchange, and for a time, it was. That was until I found out I was pregnant with you. I worried so much throughout that pregnancy. I spent the whole nine months waiting for the sea witch to jump out and claim what was hers. When you were born, the fear only got worse. I begged your father to move inland, but he refused, saying that this was his ancestral home and the royal palace. I couldn't tell him why I wanted to move. I was scared he'd hate me if he found out what I was."

She wiped her eyes with the handkerchief and carried on, her voice barely more than a whisper.

"Instead, I developed a fear of the ocean. I'd not been back in such a long time; it was an easy fear to make up. The irony was that the place I'd come from, the place I'd grown up in was now my greatest fear. I kept you, and when your brother came along, him too, away from the sea. I've spent the last eighteen years being terrified she would come and take you away from me."

"Why didn't she?"

"She's tied to the ocean like the rest of us are. It takes a great deal of magic to give people legs, and she only gives if she can take more back. The few merfolk that have come onto land have stayed here. She is too important down below to leave, although I know she craves it. She has been biding her time until you step foot in there. I hoped that would never happen, but then you jumped onto that boat."

I thought back to the sound of my mother's screams as I fell into the water on the day the *Erica Rose* sank. Knowing what I knew now, I felt sick at what I'd done. If only my mother had told me the truth long ago.

"She appeared almost straight away," my mother continued. "I don't know how, but I believe she could sense you. I saw the black shape in the water coming right for you. Everyone else thought it was a particularly bad storm, but storms don't look like that. It was the witch that brought the *Erica Rose* down."

She sniffed. "It's funny. Everyone else was worried that you'd drown. I was almost hoping you would. Anything would be better than being taken by the witch. She takes of you what she can and leaves you with nothing. No bargain or exchange with her works out well for the person doing it, no matter how good she makes it seem. In exchange for my legs and my life up here, I have spent the last eighteen years in fear."

I could see the tears welling in her eyes again. This was so difficult, and my heart was breaking for her. To have kept all this a secret for so many years. The shadow she lived under must have been terrible.

"When I heard that you'd been found alive and had been brought back here after the *Erica Rose* sank, I was so happy. That was until you told me who had saved you. I didn't know who it was, but the way you described him, I knew straight away it was a merman. I could see it in your eyes that he'd made an impression on you. That's why I tried to tell you that you'd imagined it. I hoped that you'd pass it off as a hallucination, but you didn't let it go.

"The night of the ball I saw you kissing him. I knew it was him straight away. The mermen all have long hair, but I've yet to see it in a male land dweller.

"It was then that I convinced your father to announce your engagement to Hayden. I told him it was the right thing to do. He was skeptical, but I was insistent. He works away from home so often, making royal visits and such, that it was easy to tell him this thing between you and Hayden was real. I just had to convince you of the same thing. It didn't work, though, did it? You were already besotted with someone else. I could see it in your eyes."

I sighed. "I've never had any interest in Hayden that way." I wanted to ask how the wedding had gone, but that story was for another time. I had to know what happened next.

"I know. I've always known. I was trying to protect you. I hoped that marrying Hayden would put an end to all this with the merman, but I can see that it won't. The thing is, you can't be with him. I don't know how she didn't catch you that time you visited him in the ocean, but you saw her today. If I'd not had all the guards out on the ocean as soon as I saw that Astrid wasn't you, she would have gotten you. I have no idea what she intends to do with you, but I know it won't be nice. I've seen her cut off girls' hair and keep them as slaves. I've known her to kill for just one drop of blood for her potions. I can't let that happen to you."

She dissolved into tears again.

My mind whirled at all this new information. It explained so much. My overwhelming love of the sea despite never having been in it. It was because I was half mermaid. My long hair, too red to be natural, was nothing like anyone else's I'd ever seen, and even though I didn't have the flecks of purple that Ari had or that my mother had shown tonight, I did have bright green eyes.

It also explained my mother's morbid fear of the water, of why she had kept both Anthony and me away from it. She wasn't scared we'd drown, she was scared the sea witch would take us. If the witch couldn't get me, it made sense she'd go for Anthony.

I hugged my mother tightly. I'd never felt close to her. I felt like the barrier between us had finally come down. Now, I knew what she was and what I was. For the first time, she felt like the mother I'd always wanted. I knew we had a long way to go, but if anything good had come out of this mess, a better relationship with my mother was all I could hope for.

My thoughts turned to Ari. I'd thought he had just decided not to turn up. I'd thought he'd gotten cold feet, but if what my mother said was true, another, much worse thought came to me.

"Ari, the merman had legs the night of the ball. Do you think he was able to do that because of the sea witch?"

She gave a long sigh. "Undoubtedly. There is no way he would be able to walk without her help. I'm surprised she let him have his tail back afterward, but I guess he's willing to offer her more than I was."

"More than your firstborn child? What more could he offer than that?"

"I don't know, but the fact that he didn't come for you tonight tells me that she didn't get what she wanted. I'm so sorry, Erica, but she must have taken him instead."

The sea witch

My heart sank as I took in the implications of her words. A few minutes ago, I'd thought that the worst thing in the world to happen to me was to be stood up by Ari. But I'd take that over him being kidnapped by a sea witch who liked to kill people any time she felt like it.

"We have to go rescue him," I said, standing up from the bed.

My mother adopted a look of horror.

"We can't! You can't! I told you how powerful she is. Everyone under the water is afraid of her. My own parents refused to have anything to do with her."

"I thought your parents were dead?"

My mother bowed her head. "They are alive. I haven't seen them in twenty years. Once I was out of the ocean, I couldn't ever go back. They don't know where I am. If I'd told them, they would never have let me come."

I shook my head. This secrecy had been going on long enough. My poor mother had spun herself such a web of lies, that now, she was the one coming unraveled.

"I can't leave him out there. He saved my life. If it weren't for him, we wouldn't be here having this conversation."

"I know," she replied. "But we can't beat her. Our only way to stay safe is to stay away from her, to stay on land. The second we go into the sea, she will be upon us and I doubt she'd let you get away again."

I thought of a way around it. "What if we don't go in the sea? Hayden's father is an admiral of the Navy. He has a whole fleet of ships. We send them all out to sea and find him that way."

"I think your father might notice all the naval ships leaving."

"So, we tell him why. It's been long enough. Don't you think he deserves to know the truth?" I cried, feeling exasperated.

My mother's jaw tightened. "No, I don't. You don't understand. The merpeople and the land dwellers don't mix. Why do you think we hide from them? History has told us that once a merperson is found, the land dwellers capture them and give them to scientists to examine. If that happened to me...or to you or Anthony, what do you think they'll do? It would be worse than being at the mercy of the sea witch. They'd cut us up to study our anatomy or keep us captive for our entire lives. Do you want that?"

"No, but I'm only talking about telling father and your best friends. I'm not suggesting we broadcast it on the evening news. Father won't give us away, neither will the Harrington-Blythes."

"Do you want to bet your life on it?" she looked at me in such a way that I knew she was being serious.

"No, but..."

She cut me off. "Everyone will see the naval ships going out. They'll wonder what is going on. We already have almost all the journalists in the kingdom camping on our doorsteps because of this wedding fiasco. Do you really want to give them something else to write about?"

Oh, the wedding. I'd forgotten about that. I thought of Hayden and Astrid downstairs. As the pair of them came to mind, a plan began to form. Whatever had happened down there today, I figured they owed me. I might have made a giant mess of the day, but because of that, Hayden wasn't tied to me for the rest of his life. Surely, that must count for something...?

"Hayden has a boat," I said out loud, suddenly feeling excited. "He is also an excellent sailor, thanks to his father, and I know Astrid is a great swimmer."

"Hayden has a boat barely bigger than a dingy that seats four people and being a great swimmer counts for nothing when the sea witch gets to you. You saw what she does. If she can sink a ship as grand as the *Erica Rose*, what chance does Hayden's dingy stand? None at all!"

"Maybe not, but it's all we have. I refuse to stand by and let Ari get hurt just because you don't want the truth to come out. I'm going back out into the ocean tonight."

She opened her mouth as if to say something and then closed it again, obviously deciding against it. I didn't want to blackmail her into letting us go by threatening to tell my father her secret. Thankfully, she just nodded her head.

"If you must go, I know I will not be able to stop you. I've done everything in my power to keep you from the ocean, and you've found a way around me every time. I hate that you are doing this, but beyond keeping you locked in your room for eternity, I see no way around it. I knew this day would come eventually, and I'm tired of fighting it."

She did look tired, exhausted even. I waited for her to say more, but instead, she pulled out a long necklace from around her neck. "Please take this."

A huge red ruby glistened in the light. It hung from a gold chain. I'd seen her wear it every day of her life. She leaned toward me and placed it over my head.

"Why are you giving me this?" I asked, picking up the ruby and examining it.

"It has a protection spell on it. It has faded a lot over the years, but I'd rather you have the little protection it does possess."

I could see the tears in her eyes already beginning to form. This was her greatest fear. The day she hoped would never come. I knew that going out to sea would hurt her, but I couldn't leave Ari, not after everything he'd done for me. My heart went out to my mother then. She was letting me go despite doing everything in her power to keep me safe all these years. I was eighteen now, an adult, and I guess she knew deep down that she couldn't stop me. I leaned forward and hugged her tightly. A part of me never wanted to let her go.

She must have felt the same way because we stayed like that for nearly five minutes.

"I'll speak to your father and sort out the wedding fiasco," she said, finally pulling away from me. She wiped her tears and pulled a lipstick from her pocket reapplied it using a pocket mirror as a guide.

"What will you say?" I asked, wondering how I was going to get away with this.

She gave me a brief smile. "I'm the queen. I'll think of something. I should come down with you, though. We've gotten rid of the media, but I know Hayden's parents will want answers."

Hayden's parents. I wondered if they hated me for what I'd done or if they were secretly happy. After all, they didn't particularly want their son to marry me. They were blackmailed into it.

I followed my mother down the stairs. She walked so slowly, so deliberately as she always did, appearing regal at all times. It was killing me not to run past her, to get to the sea quickly, but I'd never make it out of the palace without her help, so I had to follow in her footsteps and walk at the pace she set.

At the bottom of the stairs, she ordered one of the guards to get Hayden's boat ready to sail. He nodded his head curtly and left through one of the doors.

Everyone's eyes turned to us as we opened the main hall doors.

"I'd like a word with Hayden and Astrid if you don't mind," she said to the assembled group of people.

Hayden stood, and Astrid looked toward us in surprise.

My mother beckoned my friends toward us. "Come on, quickly. I have a job I'd like you to help me with."

Now, it was my father's turn to look surprised. "What's going on, Delilah?"

My mother smiled, but she kept waving her hands impatiently. "It's not important; I'll tell you later. I'd just like these two to help me with something if they don't mind."

Both Astrid and Hayden crossed the great hall with confused expressions on their faces. As soon as they had walked through the door, my mother closed it behind us.

"What's going on?" asked Hayden. He was still in his wedding suit. His usually messy hair was combed straight, and he wore a white rose in his lapel. He looked so handsome.

"No time to explain. Come with me quickly, you too, Astrid."

I took off down the corridor that would lead to the back of the palace. It was a longer route than simply dashing through the main hall, but with everyone still in there, this way would have to do.

On the promenade, close to where I'd been pulled out of the boat, Hayden's boat was waiting. A couple of guards stood next to it.

"Jump in," I shouted to the others, but one of the guards stopped me.

"We've only just rescued you. I can't let you go back out to sea without consulting the king or queen."

I opened my mouth to argue, but the other guard spoke first. "This is the queen's orders. Let them go."

I jumped down into the small sailboat, quickly followed by Hayden and Astrid. Hayden pulled on a rope which cast us off the side of the promenade.

Once we were far enough away from the guards, I pointed out to the horizon. "Go that way," I ordered Hayden.

He fiddled about with the ropes, changing the position of the sails, and pretty soon, we were heading out into the deep water. I couldn't see the sea witch, but I didn't need to. I already knew she'd come for me. She had done so twice already and not caught me. I just wanted to be as far away from the coast as possible when it happened. There were still many people there, not to mention the media and I didn't want any of them to see what we were up to.

Hayden was a pro at sailing, having done it his whole life. His boat was little more than a dinghy, but I knew he could sail greater craft. One day, he would make a great captain of a ship just like his father.

"Are you going to tell us what's happening?" asked Hayden, looking confused as well he should be.

"Do you believe in magical creatures?" I asked, deciding that the truth was easier than trying to come up with something.

Hayden stopped what he was doing and turned to look at me. "Magical creatures? Have you banged your head?"

"Stop it, Hayden," admonished Astrid. "Yes, I do. There is magic in some of the other kingdoms. I've heard about it. Just because we don't have it here in Trifork, doesn't mean it doesn't exist."

"Magic, yeah," scoffed Hayden, "but magical creatures? What are we talking about here? Monsters, ghosts? Griffins? What?"

I took a deep breath and let my hand trail in the cool water. "I've told you both about the stranger I met, the one who saved me from drowning after the *Erica Rose* went down. Astrid, you've met him."

"Ari?" asked Astrid.

Hayden gave us both a strange look. "Who is Ari? Is that the guy you were dancing with on the night of your ball? The weirdo with the long hair? I wondered who he was."

"I told you who he was on the night of the ball," I said, only half lying. "I told you that I'd been rescued from the *Erica Rose*. It was Ari that saved me."

Astrid nodded. "He was the one who came to collect me from my aunt's house. He was very charming and quite the looker. He was quite strange. He refused to talk to me and only told me the plan by writing it down on paper. I didn't see anything magical about him, though."

"You wouldn't if he was on land. It's only under the sea where you can see his magic. He's a merman."

Astrid laughed, and Hayden coughed.

"He's a mermaid? Are you serious?"

I prodded him in the stomach to shut him up. "Yes, I'm serious, and no, he's not a mermaid. He's a guy."

"A guy with a fishtail," barked Hayden.

I ignored the tone in his voice and told them both the full story about how I met Ari, right through to what my mother told me in her bedroom not twenty minutes earlier.

I could tell that Hayden didn't believe me, but Astrid had a look of excitement on her face. "You mean to tell me that we are out here on a rescue mission? Oh, I wish I'd have known, I'd have brought my sword!"

I shook my head and smiled. Astrid was one of those girls who was always up for anything. She had no fear. Not many women would take the place of the royal princess at the wedding, and fewer still would get excited at the prospect of battling a sea witch.

The boat began to rock slightly, and my fingers in the water turned colder. Sitting up, I looked over the side. All around us the water was the color of night. The sea witch had found me.

Body parts

"Ok, I believe you," said Hayden, pulling me back to the center of the boat as it listed precariously. He pulled on a couple of ropes, and the sails came fluttering down. "What's the plan?"

"The plan is to rescue Ari."

"How?" he grumbled, gripping the side of the boat. Beneath us, the water churned like boiling oil except it was cold, much colder than the rest of the ocean. We needed to stay above the water level. If the witch managed to pull us under, then it would be over for us.

"I don't know," I admitted. I'd not really thought further than coming out here. But the problem was, we were on top of the water and Ari, as far as I knew, was below it. Without his help, none of us could breathe underwater, and to top it all off, I still couldn't swim. "I'm sorry."

Hayden rolled his eyes at me and slashed at the water with his hands. I wasn't sure what he was aiming to do, but it was having no effect other than to splash us all. Why hadn't I thought to bring a gun? I had no idea where I'd get a gun, but to come out here with no plan and no weapons was stupid.

The boat began to float quickly. It was as if it was being pulled by an invisible force. The sails were down. The only thing pulling us was the sea witch. It picked up speed, and I noticed it was going around in a wide circle.

"It's a whirlpool," Astrid screamed, her eyes wide with fear as she looked out over the side. I followed her gaze and saw the most terrifying thing I'd ever seen. It was as if someone had pulled a plug out of the ocean floor. The water was spiraling downwards right into the inky blackness, and we were on course to fall into it. As we circled closer and closer to the vortex, the small boat creaked under the pressure. We were spinning quickly like waltzers at a fairground, and the clouds above us were just a blur as we fell right into the hole.

Once we had circled almost to the seabed, the movement stopped. The boat hit the sandy seabed with a thump, and for a brief second, we were still. Far above us, I could see the sky. And then it happened—the sea came crashing in around us. I was washed right out of the boat, and no amount of trying to swim would help. I rolled in all directions, being buffeted by the onslaught of water so dark, I couldn't even see my fingertips.

I wasn't even scared. I was annoyed. Annoyed that I was once again drowning because of stupidity and recklessness. Almost as soon as it started, it stopped. The water cleared, and I fell through it to the seabed. Beneath me, soft sand cushioned my fall. I got to my feet quickly and much more easily than I expected, considering the force of the water above me. Sun filtered through a wide hole above me, allowing me to see. Hayden was lying on the ground, untangling himself from a bed of seaweed. Just behind him, I saw Astrid looking about her wide-eyed. When she caught me looking at her, she put her thumbs up to show me she was ok.

A loud voice boomed out behind us causing me to turn quickly.

The sea witch stood in all her glory, towering above us. Her skin, purple with shades of green that reminded me of my dress for the ball. But unlike my dress, the green was algae or some other kind of plant growing right on her. Parts of it were healthy and pink, but they looked so strange plastered on in strips. The rest of her skin was cracked and old, but that was not what had me sucking in my breath; it was her legs. She had six of them, just like Ollie's tentacles. That, combined with her two arms, gave her the appearance of an aged octopus.

"I wondered if you would come," she cackled in a high-pitched voice. It didn't suit her at all. It was almost as though she'd borrowed it from someone else. "I've been waiting a long time for you. Fortunes told that you would be beautiful, but I must say they were rather understated. You are stunning."

I opened my mouth to speak; but before I had the chance, Astrid ran right past me and jabbed her finger in the old woman's belly. "Where is he, you rancid old crone?"

The witch glanced down at Astrid, who was half her size, at most.

"What beautiful blonde hair you have," she drawled. "I always wanted to be a blonde." With a wave of her hand, Astrid's hair began to turn black, then purple and green, and then fell out in clumps until it was a matted patchy mess on top of her head. The beautiful long blonde locks she was so proud of appeared on the old witch's head by way of magic.

"There, that's a nice swap, don't you think?" She waved her hand again, and Astrid was pushed back into the water against a wall.

It was then I realized we were in a cave. We were still underwater, but we were speaking and breathing as normal. The whole effect was disconcerting because I could feel the water, but it had no effect on us.

Hayden ran past me toward the old woman, but he too was sent flying into the walls.

They were both unconscious. My backup was gone. It was just me and the witch, and she had the advantage. She was double my size and knew magic. I didn't even have a weapon.

I wasn't about to back down without a fight, though. I'd come here to get Ari, and I wasn't going to leave without him.

"Where is he?" I demanded, putting my hands on my hips, although keeping the distance between us. I wasn't sure how powerful she was, but I wasn't going to make it easy on her.

"Run away!" I heard him shout. I looked quickly from side to side, trying to see him. *"It's a trap. She used me for bait. She only wants you."*

I looked around again. Where was he? The dark cave, illuminated with an ethereal green glow, had no hiding places. A few hardy sea plants grew down here, but there was no other sign of life. And then I saw it. A sight so horrific it made my stomach lurch. Right at the back of the cave a line of men were shackled to the wall. More correctly, they once had been men. Parts of their bodies were missing, strips of skin pulled from them. None of them were alive. I recognized them as the crew of the *Erica Rose*.

"They were pretty useless, being men," she said upon seeing what had grabbed my attention. "I took some bits of skin from them, but there was little else I could use. Their voices were way too manly for my pretty face."

I hoped she was joking. I'd never seen an uglier-looking woman in my whole life.

"I took their voices anyway. I had to, to shut them up. The sound of them begging for their lives was just too much."

She turned back to me. I had to take a deep breath so as not to lose my lunch.

"I never thought this day would come," she gloated, taking a step toward me. The way she walked on her six legs looked strange and awkward. Inadvertently, I took a step back. There was no use pretending I wasn't petrified.

"Where are you?" I asked. If I could hear him, it meant he was close; and if he was nearby, it meant I had a chance of helping him escape.

"I'm here. The witch has used a spell on me. I'm invisible."

"Where?" I asked again. I didn't want to look around too much in case the witch realized we were communicating.

"I've waited for so long to finally meet you and take what's mine," she said, completely oblivious to the in-head conversation I was having with Ari.

She pushed herself up from the ground and swam toward me, displacing the sand beneath her as she did. She was much more graceful at swimming than she was at walking.

"I'm to your right. Can you see the shackles on the wall? That's where I am."

I cast my eyes to the side quickly. The shackles were just a couple of feet away from Hayden, who was just beginning to stir. If only I could communicate with him too.

"Hayden, can you hear me?"

The witch got closer and closer. I backed up until I hit a wall. The only way I could see to get out of here was a hole in the ceiling that led to the open ocean. With the witch's strange magic surrounding us, I wasn't even sure I would be able to swim. Even though I could feel the water around me, my movements were normal. Walking backward was easy with no resistance. It was almost as though the water was a hallucination. I certainly didn't feel wet.

"He can't hear you. It's a complicated thing I should have explained to you before. Only I can hear you. Don't let her touch you. You saw her

take your friend's hair. She'll want something else from you."

I already knew what she wanted from me. I thought back to what my mother had told me in her bedroom. She wanted my legs. The thing she gave my mother she wanted back. I could see it now. The witch looked odd because she was cobbled together of different parts. Her hair sparkled a perfect pale blonde, fresh and new. Her hands were the hands of an old woman with gold rings adorning every finger and thumb. The rest of her was grotesque and the closer she got, the worse she looked.

Her dull skin was flaky and her eyes a dull seaweed brown. She got right up to me and pulled back thin lips coated in some kind of unevenly applied purple lipstick. When she did, I saw yellowing teeth, crumbling from age.

"What do I do?" I shouted, forgetting I was supposed to be speaking in my head.

Over her shoulder, I saw Hayden stand. He'd woken up. He had a cut on the side of his head where he'd hit the wall and streaks of blood floated weirdly around him. He picked up a piece of wood, which I realized was part of the boat we'd been in and raised it as if to hit the witch over the head.

I tried not to look at him as he came closer. I didn't want a flicker of my eyes to give him away, but it wasn't enough. She pushed her hand behind her sending him jettisoning into the wall once again, this time, knocking him out completely.

"Let us go!" I shouted with as much anger as I could muster. Inside my heart was pounding, but I'd been well schooled on the art of hiding one's emotions. She could see my anger, but I wasn't going to show her my fear.

She laughed, a long, low cackle. She was enjoying this. It wasn't enough that she wanted to take my legs, she wanted to enjoy the experience.

"I'll let your friends go if you like. I have all I need with you anyway." She looked me up and down and cackled again. With a wave of her hand the whirlpool started again, but this time it was dragging everything upwards. Hayden and Astrid began to spin. As both of them were unconscious, they couldn't even try to swim against it.

"If they go through that hole, the magic won't work," I shouted. "Without a merperson holding them, they won't be able to breathe."

I pushed the Witch to the side to try to grab them, but she was too quick and too strong. She grabbed my arms and forced me to watch as my two best friends circled upwards out of the hole.

"They'll drown!" I screamed, but she didn't care. She laughed again as she spun me around.

"After all these years," she hummed to herself.

I pulled against her, but the more I pulled, the harder she gripped. Her painted red nails and gold rings dug into my skin as I fought to pull loose.

"And now, your legs, I think. I'll start with those, and we'll move on up from there. You have such a pretty face; I don't think I'll want to waste a single part of you." She raised her hand again. She'd taken my friends lives and now was going to take my legs, and there was nothing I could do to stop her.

I pushed my legs up against her to try and push away, but that only helped her. She grabbed one and began to perform the spell. I tried to swim away, but swimming was impossible in the strange environment.

Struggling, I turned back to her, and as I did, one of her rings ripped my t-shirt.

Her eyes went wide. Ear-piercing screams filled the room. She was so loud that everything began to rumble.

She shot back away from me so quickly that I barely had time to register that I was free before water, real water this time, began flooding into the cave. The witch had vanished into thin air

Water came crashing down on top of me, the kind I couldn't breathe through, and knocked me into the cave wall. Trying to swim through the current was impossible. It was too strong. I could wait until the cave filled up entirely and swim through the hole in the roof, but then what? I couldn't really swim at all. Out in the open ocean, I'd be dead within minutes. I hadn't succumbed to the sea witch, but it looked like I was going to succumb to the sea.

Escape

I felt a hand grip mine. I couldn't see who it was thanks to the water battering down on me, but as I was pulled upwards at high speed, I knew it was Ari.

"Find Hayden and Astrid!" I shouted mentally to him as we passed through the opening and out into the ocean. Salt water made me blink, but I kept my eyes open.

Without any warning, Ari sped up, taking us in a different direction. I soon realized why. Both Hayden and Astrid were floating a couple of hundred feet from where we were.

No, not floating. Astrid was swimming. She must have woken up as she hit the real water. She was trying to pull the unconscious Hayden to the surface.

I looked up. They still seemed so far away. With an incredible burst of speed, Ari pulled me along through the water. He grabbed a surprised Astrid's hand and gestured for me to hold Hayden too. As soon as I caught hold of Hayden's free hand, Ari swam up to the surface. Like a rocket ship on launch, we blasted through the water, leaping high into the air before we all fell back down with a splash.

Ari pulled me back to the surface where we met Astrid and Hayden. Hayden had woken up and was now coughing up water as Astrid hit his back.

"What did you do?" I asked Ari once I could see that Hayden was alright. We all floated there in the middle of the ocean, the coast barely visible in the distance.

"I didn't do anything. I don't know what happened. One minute she was going for your legs, the next the magic shackles fell off, and water was pouring in through the ceiling. I think we should get you all home before she comes back."

I nodded. I didn't know what it was that had startled her, but I didn't want to hang around to find out.

The easiest way to get back to shore was to lie on the surface of the water and hold hands like a chain. Ari then pulled us swiftly back to the coastline where we ended up on a desolate beach. I recognized it immediately as the beach where we first met.

"Why didn't you take us home?" I asked, pulling myself onto the land. Ari followed, pulling himself up the sand using his strong arms. I couldn't keep my eyes off his tail. I'd seen it before, but here on land it looked strange as though it didn't belong, which made sense because it didn't

"It will turn into legs as soon as it dries," he said catching my glance.

I blushed wondering how obvious I'd been.

"I brought you here because there are a few things to discuss before we take you home. First of all, how are your parents going to react, knowing it wasn't you getting married?"

"They know. I've already been home. The sea witch came for me except I didn't know it was the sea witch then. A couple of guards saved me, but then my mother told me something. I should probably tell you too."

"Who are you talking to?" asked Astrid, looking confused.

"I'm answering Ari, who do you think?"

"She can't hear me. I'm still talking to you in your mind."

I thought for a second. So he was. I'd gotten so used to it that I'd not even noticed. I'd been answering questions out loud that Hayden and Astrid couldn't hear.

"So talk then. I think we all need to hear everything."

He looked down. Something was bothering him. I could feel it. As I waited for him to say something, his tail began to change. His face contorted into an expression of agony and his bones and skin separated into two legs.

I watched, unable to help as he gritted his teeth and closed his eyes. It hadn't occurred to me that it would hurt, changing between the sea and the land, but this transition was brutal.

I grabbed his hand and held it tightly, willing the pain away from him.

When he'd finished, he collapsed onto the beach, his breath coming in rapid bursts. I held onto his hand until he'd finally calmed down.

He was completely naked, face down on the beach. Hayden pulled his trousers off and threw them to Ari. Ari smiled, but I could still see the pain in his eyes. How long would he hurt, now that the transition was complete? With horror, I realized he'd have to go through it again to swim us back to the palace.

"Your friends can't hear me because I can't talk, and I can't talk because I had to give something in exchange for my legs."

"What do you mean?" I asked aloud, but I already knew. Ari had gone to the sea witch and asked for legs just as my mother had all those years ago. In exchange, my mother had offered up her firstborn child. Ari had given his voice. She'd taken it even though she wasn't using it.

"I knew I had to see you again. That moment on the beach after I saved you and you asked me to kiss you again...I'd thought it was funny, that maybe you'd hit your head too hard. But you looked at me so earnestly that I realized I did want to kiss you. When you left, I couldn't stop thinking of you."

I could see the other two watching us out of the corner of my eye. They were probably wondering what was going on, why I was staring at Ari without either of us talking.

"You already know that, but what you don't know is that I went to the sea witch. I knew I shouldn't have. I knew she was dangerous. But I needed to see you again so badly, and I couldn't think of another way."

"She offered you legs for your voice."

I heard Astrid say Ah as she suddenly figured out what was happening.

Ari nodded and gave me a smile that damn near broke my heart. He'd given up his voice for me.

"She gave me the ability to dance. It was not something I'd done before. We don't dance underwater, not the same way the land dwellers do. I guess she recovered quickly from whatever happened back there because I've never had this pain before. She's used her magic on me to cause my legs to hurt. It's her way of getting back at us. She must have cast the spell as we were making our escape."

I looked down at his legs. Now covered with Hayden's trousers, they looked so ordinary.

I took a couple of deep breaths and tried not to let the tears win. He'd put himself through this for me. I pulled up the bottom of his trouser leg and rubbed his calf softly. It had soft hair on it, dark, the same color as the hair on his head.

I willed his pain away from him. But each time I touched him, no matter how lightly, he winced at the slightest pressure. I laid his leg back down in the soft sand.

I thought back to the dance we'd shared the night of the ball. He'd danced beautifully. It was all part of the witch's magic.

"Can someone tell me what's going on?" asked Hayden standing up, a look of annoyance on his face. "Because I've had just about enough for one day."

I nodded. He was right. *"We should go before the sea witch comes back."*

I looked out at the fading blue light for signs of the sea witch. The black water that followed her around was nowhere to be seen, but soon it would be dark, and all the water would be black.

"Not yet," argued Ari. *"What about the wedding? Do you still have to get married?"* As he said it, his eyes wandered over to Hayden. So that was the real reason he'd brought us to this beach. It wasn't to tell me about his legs, although that might have been part of it. He wanted to know that everything he'd done had not been in vain. He wanted to know that I wasn't destined to be someone else's.

I turned to Astrid. Her veil was long gone, but she was still wearing the wedding dress. It was now a dirty grey color and was covered in sand. I tried not to think of all the time and money my mother had put into having the best seamstresses in the kingdom found to make it for me. Now, it looked no better than a rag.

"What happened at the wedding?" I asked them both. Hayden looked at me in disgust and sat down on the sand.

"We didn't get married," Astrid replied, looking up at Hayden. She lifted her hand and took his, all the while looking up at him lovingly.

"When Astrid lifted that veil, I nearly had a heart attack, but that was nothing compared to your mother. I'm surprised you didn't hear her screaming," huffed Hayden

"I did," I answered ruefully, remembering her screams over the loudspeakers. I turned to Astrid. "Why didn't you wait until the end of the ceremony. That way, you would be married now."

She sighed and began to draw small circles in the sand. "I wanted to. I almost did. But then, I'd wonder for the rest of my life if Hayden married me because he wanted to or because he was tricked into it. I want a real proposal."

"So does that mean you will have to marry him?"

I turned back to Ari. Fear was etched onto his face. I'd never had anyone look at me the way he did right then, as though I could crush his very soul with one word. I desperately wanted to bridge the distance between us and kiss him, but now was not the time. Instead, I shook my head. When I replied to him, I kept the words in my head. I didn't want the others to hear this.

"*I'm not going to marry Hayden. I've spoken to my mother, and she understands. I wouldn't have gone through with it anyway. I couldn't marry him.*"

"*Why not?*"

"*Because I'm in love with someone else.*"

He exhaled quickly and bit his lip. My blood pumped just a little bit quicker with that gesture.

"Guys, it's getting dark." Astrid stood up and peered out to sea.

"We should go," I echoed. "I've been chased by the sea witch twice today. I don't want to make it a third time."

Ari stood up and walked the few steps to the water's edge. "*The main beach is just around that cliff there. I can get us there in less than two minutes. It would take the sea witch longer to get to us. I'll swim us all along the shallows until we get back to the palace. If she does come looking, we will have to get out onto the beach.*" He jumped into the water and dove under. Seconds later, Hayden's trousers came floating up. I waded out to get them and passed them back to Hayden. Ari resurfaced and took my hand. With my other hand, I held onto Astrid, and she held onto Hayden.

I was beginning to feel more at home under the sea. Below us, small sea creatures floated by and the last trickles of daylight filtered through, creating an eerie but dazzling rippling effect. I kept my eyes out for the dark water, but Ari was right. She didn't come for us. Whatever had happened to her in her cave had stopped her in her tracks. I hoped it would stop her for good, but I knew she would be back. Now, not only had my mother gotten away from her, I had too.

Ari brought us to the small dock where Hayden, Astrid, and I had set out a couple of hours earlier. As we pulled ourselves out of the water, I heard my mother shouting my name. I looked up to see her on the balcony waving down at me. She had such a look of relief on her face. I guessed she'd been out there waiting for me the whole time. She began to run down the walkway to greet us, a pair of binoculars bobbing around her neck on a strap.

Without legs, Ari couldn't get out, so I bent forward and grabbed his hand to pull him out. Astrid did the same with his other hand. The necklace my mother had given me fell out from my top and hit Ari in the face.

"I'm sorry," I giggled as he slipped onto the promenade.

He looked up at me with a grin on his face to share the joke, but when he saw the necklace, his eyes went wide.

"I think I finally know what happened to the sea witch."

The truth about Delilah

"Oh, thank goodness you are alright." My mother barreled down the walkway and flung herself at me almost knocking me back into the water. She was still wearing the pretty dress she'd picked out for my wedding, but her hair was now out of the elaborate up-do and flowed freely. She passed us a towel each. "Come inside, all of you."

It was so strange to see my mother use so much emotion. I still couldn't get used to it. Once Ari's tail had turned back to legs and he'd been brought a pair of trousers, we followed mother back inside using a side entrance that was rarely used. I thought she would take us to the main part of the house, but she ushered us all into her drawing room. The room itself was decorated in pretty pinks and soft greys and looked completely different from the grandeur of the rest of the palace. She had a small, ornately carved writing desk that my father had inherited from one of his ancestors, but she rarely used it. She came in here for solitude, to sew or to read, away from the hustle and bustle of the palace. No members of staff were allowed in here. She called it her fortress and had to make do with cleaning it herself.

Along one wall was a floral sofa that we all fell down on. Ari grimaced as he bent his knees. It was awful knowing how much pain he was in and not being able to do a damn thing about it.

My mother pulled up a matching chair and sat opposite us.

"Your Majesty," said Ari nodding his head.

He was speaking with his mind again. I waited for her to answer, but she didn't appear to hear him. I thought that with them both being merpeople, she would be able to communicate with him through her mind. As she ignored him, I decided to speak for him.

"Ari says Your Highness," It wasn't strictly true, but he'd made the mistake so many others do. As the ruler, it was only my father that should be referred to as Your Majesty. My mother should properly be addressed as Your Highness.

She nodded back at him and turned to me.

"I'm so glad that you are back safely."

Before I had time to speak, Ari's words cut through my mind. *"The Havfrue Ruby saved you."*

I gave him a cursory glance, wondering what he knew. I decided telling my mother might bring the answers about faster.

"Ari says the Havfrue Ruby saved me. Do you know what he's talking about?"

My mother heaved a long sigh and cupped her head in her hands. I waited patiently for her to look up and tell me what was going on.

When she did, she reached forward and took hold of the ruby that was still hanging from my neck. I let her lift the necklace over my head. She'd told me it would protect me, but how did Ari know about it?

"I didn't know just how well it would work," she said addressing Ari, "although it didn't save her. I don't know how much magic it still contains. My father gave it to me to make a wish with, but I can see that it has not been used. It still has magic in it. I guess the witch saw it for what it was and was scared off. I doubt it will work again if she finds out that nothing happened to her. It was sheer dumb luck that you all survived." She walked around the room, wringing her hands together as she spoke, twisting the gold chain between her fingers. She turned back to Ari. "I didn't want her to go at all, but I know how stubborn she is. She'd only have found another way to go out to sea if I didn't let her. These last few hours have been the worst of my entire life. I've spent the whole time on that balcony waiting for you to come back. Well, in all honesty, that's not true. I was waiting for Erica, Hayden, and Astrid to come back. I hoped they wouldn't find you."

I gasped. My mother had been acting strange for the past couple of weeks, but it wasn't like her to be rude.

"How is he?" she asked, still looking at Ari. "Is he still mad?"

Now, I really didn't know what was going on. Who was she talking about?

Ari smiled and took her hand, obviously not put off by her rudeness. *"He never truly recovered."*

"He never recovered," I repeated back what Ari had said so my mother could hear.

Tears began to prick the corners of her eyes. I looked around to Hayden and Astrid to see if they had any more of a clue than I, but they looked as dumbfounded as I felt. At least, Astrid did. Hayden just sat there with a grimace on his face.

"Please, can one of you tell me what is going on?" I asked, feeling frustrated. "Do you two know each other?"

My mother closed her eyes and sighed again, looking utterly defeated. "You tell her."

Ari turned to me. *"When I came here to the ball, I didn't pay attention to the king and queen. I didn't really pay attention to anyone but you. As you know, I was only inside for a few minutes before going outside to dance. If I'd have taken the time to look around me, I'd have recognized your mother. Maybe not straight away. She left before I was born, but she looks so much like some girls I know. The Havfrue Ruby confirmed for me who she is."*

"I know she's a mermaid," I said to him in my mind. *"But why would she look like those other people?"*

"Your mother isn't who you think she is. Her name is Anaitis. Those people she looks like are her sisters. Your mother is the heir to the throne of Havfrue. When her father, the king, dies, she will become queen."

"But she's already the queen of Trifork," I said rather stupidly. I looked at my mother. Tears fell down over her pale cheeks.

"You are the heir to the throne underwater as well?"

Hayden and Astrid stared at her as she nodded her head. So much emotion was overwhelming her that she didn't speak. She just cried, hiding her face in her hands.

Hayden stood up and left the room, slamming the door behind him. What was going on with him today?

"I'm sorry," I heard her mumble between her fingers.

I stood up and gave her an awkward hug. I was still getting used to this new version of my mother.

I turned to Astrid. "Please, can you get one of the palace staff to bring us some tea. I think we are going to need it."

She nodded and stood up. As she ambled to the door, my mother asked her to forget the tea and bring us all a whiskey. I guessed it was going to be one of those nights.

Ten minutes and a burning throat later, my mother was ready to talk. Her hands shook with each word she spoke. Her history was not something that was easy for her to dwell on.

"You've never met the king of Havfrue," she said, speaking to Astrid and me before turning to Ari, "But you, Ari will know what he is like. He is nothing like your father, Erica. He is a stern man, a strict man, and he rules Havfrue with an iron fist. He is fair to his subjects and is a good leader but living with him was a nightmare. My mother died when I was young, leaving me and my six sisters. I was the eldest and, as such, was expected to look after the rest of them. I didn't really mind, but my father became so overprotective of us that he stopped letting us out of his sight. If we left his side for more than a minute or failed to tell him where we were going, he became so angry."

She stood up and brought a box of tissues from her writing desk. Pulling one out, she dabbed her eyes and sat back down. Ari poured another glass of whiskey and passed it to her. She accepted it gracefully before knocking it back in one swallow.

"As you can probably tell, I was a willful child, always disobeying orders. I was in trouble all the time. In the end, I couldn't stand it anymore. You know the rest. I swam away after a particularly bad fight with my father and never went home again. I hated leaving my sisters, but after visiting the sea witch, I had to stay on land. I was not given the opportunity to return, but if I had been, I probably wouldn't have taken it. Trifork is my home now."

She hiccupped and set the glass down on the table next to her.

"Do you think she'll come back, the sea witch?" asked Astrid, running her fingers through her shaggy hair.

"She won't come on land, but she believes I owe her. If I go into the sea, or if Erica does, she will know, and she will come back. The Havfrue Ruby won't keep either of us safe for too long. You were lucky it worked the one time."

"I cannot go back either. She knows I am with you now. If I go back, she will use me to get to you like she did before."

I'd only had one glass of whiskey, but it was making my head spin. It had been an exhausting day, and I couldn't take in any more information.

"I don't know about anyone else, but I need to sleep. Let's go to bed and work this out in the morning." I yawned as if to prove my point.

"What's to work out?" asked Astrid. "We saved Ari. Your mother hasn't gone in the sea for years. Surely, Ari can stay out too."

"I guess," I said, looking towards Ari. He looked as tired as I felt. He was stuck. He couldn't go back to the sea because of me, but to stay on land meant that he'd never have a voice and would have to spend his days walking in agony. "Mother, can we find guest rooms for Ari and Astrid?"

My mother nodded her head, but the whiskey had affected her. With Ari's help, we were able to walk her up the stairs to her own bedroom. My father was already there. His voice boomed out as I knocked on his door.

"Who is it?"

"It's me, Erica. I've got mother here. I think she needs to sleep." She was propped up in our arms, her head lolling to one side. My father opened his bedroom door and took her from us.

"What's the matter with her?" he asked, looking down on her in concern.

"Too much whiskey," I said. "I think she was stressed out about today and accidentally drank too much."

My father raised an eyebrow. Drinking hard liquor was another thing my mother was not known to do. I guess neither of us knew her as well as we thought we did.

He carried her to bed and placed her down gently. I quietly closed the door before my father could ask any more questions. My mother could deal with him in the morning.

I took Astrid and Ari to the lower level where the guest rooms were. Astrid took one, and I showed Ari to another.

I wanted to kiss him, but I was so tired. My mother wasn't the only one exhausted by the day. I could barely keep my eyes open.

"We'll speak tomorrow," I said.

He looked disappointed but didn't reply.

I wearily dragged myself up to my room only to find Hayden there. "What are you doing here?" I asked, wishing he'd gone home. He'd been in a funny mood all day, and I was too tired to find out why. I just wanted to keel over and fall asleep on my bed.

"What is going on with you, Erica?" His voice had more than a hint of anger.

"What? Nothing is going on. What's going on with you? You've been looking like you've been slapped around the head with a wet kipper all day."

"Nothing? I woke up this morning expecting to be getting married, and instead, I ended up on some lunatic suicide mission for...for...for one of those."

"One of those?"

"You know what I mean. A stinking sea person." He slammed his fist down on the bed. I'd never seen him so angry before.

"Ari saved my life. I'm sorry if it bothers you that he is a merman, but it's really none of your business."

221

"That's right," he growled, "it isn't any of my business, and yet, you dragged Astrid and me out with you, knowing full well we were going right into the lair of some crazy old sea bitch."

He was right. I'd not asked if he would help or told him what I needed him for; I'd just instructed him to sail me out to sea. We'd been best friends for so long, that it hadn't occurred to me to ask him if he wanted to help me. He'd always come to my aid when I needed it in the past. Mind you, I'd never asked him to save my life before today.

"I'm sorry," I replied lamely, "I thought you'd want to help."

"And why would I want to help?" He was so cross, his voice hard and full of aggravation. I was too tired to even try to be nice anymore. I matched his tone as I answered him.

"Because we are friends. That's what friends do," I yelled back. "I thought you'd be happy today. I managed to put a stop to our wedding. You don't have to be married to me. I thought I was doing you a favor."

His face set in a grimace. "Don't give me that. You were doing yourself a favor. Just like everyone else around here, you thought it was okay to make a life-changing decision about my life without consulting me first. Well, it isn't okay." He opened the bedroom door. "It's not even close."

The door slammed behind him with a bang.

I sat on the bed wondering just what was going on with everyone. First, my mother was acting completely out of character, now Hayden.

I fell into bed and closed my eyes.

A few minutes later, I heard my door open again. I opened my eyes, hoping it wasn't Hayden back for another round.

It wasn't. It was Ari. I smiled as he sat on my bed.

"I'm so glad it's you," I smiled. The smile dropped when I saw the worried look on his face.

"What is it?" I asked, pulling myself up in bed.

"I have to tell you something," he replied. I could see the flashes of purple in his eyes despite the low light in the room.

"Okay." I patted the bed next to me. He sat and took my hand.

"It's about why your mother couldn't hear me when I spoke to you. I haven't been completely honest. I was hoping I'd never have to tell you this, but if I don't, your mother will."

"Okay," I said again, answering him with my mind. It felt weird being the only one to speak aloud, especially when he was telling me something important.

He took a deep breath. I could see how nervous he was. Whatever he was about to tell me, it was a big deal for him.

"Merpeople communicate through our minds," he began. I already knew that. We were doing just that with each other now. *"Humans don't. At first, I couldn't understand why I could talk to you like this. But when I found out who your mother was, it made sense. You are half mermaid."*

I nodded. Being called a half mermaid felt strange. Of course, I was, but it was something I would have to get used to. I couldn't even swim.

"I felt better knowing that there wasn't something...strange between us, knowing that this was happening because you had mermaid blood in you. But then your mother couldn't hear me. If anything, she should be able to hear me better than you. She is a pureblood mermaid."

"Does it matter?" I asked, wondering where he was going with this.

"At first, I didn't think so; but it's been puzzling me. I remembered being told as a child that it is only under the water we can communicate. On

224

land, we have to use our voices like anyone else. I'd completely forgotten because before now, I never had reason to come on land, and you've always been able to hear me."

"Maybe you remembered wrong?" I offered.

"No," he said, his eyes flashing pure purple. *"No, I didn't remember it incorrectly. There is something else that I'd forgotten, and it explains this. It hit me as I was heading to bed. I'd never believed it existed before, but knowing what I know now, I can't think of any other explanation."*

"Are you going to tell me what it is?" I asked, reverting to using my voice again.

"Merpeople can possess an incredible ability that land dwellers can't. It's rare, but it can happen. I've only known it to happen to two couples in my whole life. When two people are perfect for each other, soul mates, a magic can happen where they get bonded together almost like what land dwellers call marriage, but in this bonding, they can never be separated. If one leaves, the other must follow. The magic keeps them near to each other. It is a magic that goes beyond love and lust. Anyone can be attracted to another person. Anyone can fall in love. In bonding, it is only when two people are attracted to each other but are also perfect

together, that it happens. It also helps them communicate through their minds above water."

I tried to take in everything he was telling me. I could almost hear his heart pounding in his chest.

"We are bonded?"

"I think so. I knew as soon as I saw you that you were special. I just didn't realize until just now how special. It's really fucking scaring me."

I looked at him. The green hadn't yet come back to his eyes. I knew he was special too, and I couldn't deny I felt more for him than I ever thought possible.

My own heart began to race as I took in the implications.

"If I leave the country?"

"I will have to come with you."

"What if you can't?" I asked softly.

"The further we are apart from each other, the heavier our hearts will feel. At only a few hundred meters, we will barely feel it, but if we travel farther and farther to another kingdom perhaps, our pain will intensify to the point our hearts are so heavy they will no longer be able to pump blood around our bodies."

"And what If I die?" I whispered softly.

He pulled me close to him drawing me into a hug. He felt so warm next to me. My body fit perfectly in his arms. We were a perfect fit.

"If you die, I will die too."

I lay back down on the bed taking Ari with me. Neither of us said another word. We just fell asleep in each other's arms.

The next morning dawned, bringing sunlight through my window. My head hurt slightly from the whiskey, and my stomach growled. In the madness the day before, I'd completely forgotten to eat.

My eyes went straight to the other side of the bed, but Ari was already gone.

Pulling myself out of bed, I headed out to the balcony, eager to get a glimpse of the sea in this beautiful weather. I loved the view in the morning when the sun hit the sea, making it sparkle. I stepped out, fixing my eyes on the horizon as I always did, but this time, there was something different. The sea had completely vanished.

Ocean Disappearing

A scream cut through the silence. I had no idea who'd made it or where it had come from, but it was obvious why it had been made. All I could see in the distance was sand covered in seaweed, dead fish, and various other sea creatures. Midway between the horizon and the palace, the ruins of a boat reminded me of the *Erica Rose*. I squinted my eyes to see if it was my ship, but it was too far away to tell. I thought back to Joe and the captain and all the others. My heart hurt knowing how they'd all ended up.

On the very horizon, was a strip of blue that told me that the sea had not vanished completely but had gone out hundreds of meters.

I dashed from my room and crashed straight into a guard, knocking him to the floor.

"I'm so sorry, Your Highness," he apologized, even though it was I that had knocked him over. I held out my hand and helped him to his feet.

"I was just coming to fetch you. Your mother requests your presence in her study."

I nodded and thanked him.

When I got there, I was surprised to see Hayden and Astrid seated in the exact same places they'd been the night before.

Astrid smiled pleasantly, but Hayden just scowled. I'd never seen him like this before. Whatever it was that was bothering him hadn't diluted overnight.

"I called them down here," My mother answered my unasked question. "Where is Ari?"

I looked around the study wondering the very same thing myself. "I don't know. I haven't seen him this morning," I answered, perching myself on the arm of the sofa.

"I thought he'd be with you," she pointed out, the implication clear. I blushed.

"No, I put him in one of the guest rooms." I didn't tell her that we'd fallen asleep together in my bed.

"Oh," she replied brightening up slightly. "That's good. I'd hate for gossip to get around the palace."

What with everything else happening, a bit of gossip over whether I'd slept with Ari was the least of my concerns. Apparently, my mother was back to her normal self again. Prim and proper.

She adjusted her skirts and cleared her throat before beginning. "I asked you all here to thank you for yesterday. As you can imagine I was dealing with a lot. I told you all a lot of things that I'd hoped I'd take to the grave with me, and though I hate to do this, I'm asking you to keep those secrets."

I noticed Hayden screw up his nose as if she'd asked him to do something terrible. Thankfully, my mother didn't notice.

"Don't you think that father might notice that the sea is gone?" I asked before Hayden could jump in. Just because I understood that he was in a bad mood didn't mean I wanted him to upset my mother.

She shook her head. "He knows. I told him about the sea witch and everything that happened yesterday. I just left out my involvement. He thinks it's because of Ari."

My eyes goggled. "You are blaming Ari for all this?"

She looked straight at me. "Well, technically, it is his fault. None of this would have happened if he'd stayed under the water where he belonged."

"That's a bit rich, considering." I stood up, anger rising within me. This had all begun when she decided to leave Havfrue all those years ago. Anything that happened since was just a consequence of that.

"I know, I know," she acknowledged, flapping her arms at me to get me to sit back down. "I shouldn't have said it. It was this morning, and I'm afraid I was a little bit worse for wear, thanks to the whiskey. It just came out. As soon as my head cleared, and I thought about what I'd done, I realized I wasn't being fair."

She looked so embarrassed with herself. After so many years of keeping her heritage secret, now that it had come to light, she didn't know what to do with herself.

"What are you going to do to rectify it?" I questioned.

She sighed and raised her hand to her head. No doubt, the after-effects of last night's drinking session hadn't quite left her. "I'll have a talk with your father and tell him that I heard that the sea witch was going to do this anyway. I think he wants to get the navy out, but I'm not sure how, considering there is no sea to sail the ships on."

"That's a great idea!" Hayden agreed, standing up. "My father will sort this out. We can't have Trifork held hostage by any underwater adversaries. We need to deal with the problem swiftly."

"Where are you going?" asked Astrid as he strode right past her and headed for the door.

He pulled his features into a sneer that didn't suit him. "I think it's about time I helped out on that front. After all, if my father thinks I'm old enough to get married, he'll surely think I'm able to join the naval fleet." He opened the door and left, leaving the three of us stunned.

"Did he just say he was going to join the navy?" asked Astrid, although she knew that's exactly what he'd said.

What she didn't know was that when he talked of our enemies, it wasn't the sea witch he was referring to. He'd made it very clear last night that he had a problem with the merpeople. What he hadn't made clear was why.

I stood up quickly

"Where is my father?" I asked.

My mother waved her hand upwards. "He's upstairs with Hayden's father planning a strategy I think. I promise I'll go speak to him soon."

I turned to leave. As the door closed behind me, I heard my mother assuring Astrid that Hayden would make a fine sailor. I'm not exactly sure that's what Astrid wanted to hear.

I stomped upstairs to the main part of the palace and knocked on my father's conference room door. Inside, was a huge oval table with chairs reserved for the kingdom's highest dignitaries. I was surprised to see Ari sitting in one of the chairs next to my father. At my father's other side sat Admiral Harrington-Smyth.

My father looked up as the door closed behind me. "Ah, Erica. Come in. You didn't tell me you had a friend staying over. Is this the reason you took off yesterday?"

I stared at them open-mouthed. I'd expected to see Hayden, not Ari

"Don't worry. I'm not upset. Neither is the admiral here," continued my father, mistaking my shock as worry over the wedding. That already felt like a hundred years ago. It was all your mother's idea, really, and she doesn't seem to care today. Have you seen her, by the way? She's all over the place lately. She seemed to think that it was this chap's fault that the sea disappeared, but I think that was the whiskey talking."

"She's in her study with Astrid," I replied. "Did Hayden just come up here?"

"He did indeed. Just walked in and then turned back around and walked out without saying anything. He probably forgot what he wanted. I do that all the time."

He nudged Hayden's father with his elbow and gave him a jovial smile before turning back to me. "Come on, what are you dilly-dallying over? Come and sit beside Ari here. He's a quiet fellow, but he seems to think that we can defeat this sea witch person your mother talked about."

I was going to ask how he knew that, but I could see a pad of paper with writing on it and a pen next to it. I raised an eyebrow, and he grinned back.

Taking the seat my father pointed out, I tried to make out what had already been said by reading Ari's writing on the notepad. My father poured over sea charts as I leaned forward.

"Where is this?" he asked Ari jabbing his finger at the map. It all looked like sea to me.

Ari pulled the pad towards him, scribbled something down and passed it back to my father.

He picked it up and held it to his face, his eyesight not being as good as it could have been.

He read whatever Ari had written then peered over the notebook at me.

"I must say, I was surprised when this young chap brazenly walked in here this morning, but when he told me he was friends with you and knew where the sea witch lived, I let him stay."

Ari grinned again. The whole world had gone mad. First, my mother went crazy and told me she is a mermaid. Then, Hayden got a stick up his butt over the merpeople or the wedding, I still wasn't sure which. And now, my father had let Ari into his most private room. The room where important decisions about the kingdom were discussed, and almost no one was allowed to enter, not usually anyway. My head reeled from everything going on

"Does he know you are a merman?" I asked Ari in my head.

"No. He does know we exist, though. He told me a story about how his ancestors had trouble with the men of the sea over a hundred years ago. After a brief war, they decided it was best to keep to their own kingdoms and never cross paths again. It seems the people of Trifork have almost forgotten we exist. The people of Havfrue

have been harboring a grudge about it for all this time."

"Oh, young love," my father nudged his long-suffering friend again and pointed his eyes towards us. "Gazing into each other's eyes. I knew young Hayden wasn't right for you, no offence, Henry. There must be something in the air at the moment."

"Daddy!" I chastised, feeling more and more uncomfortable with each passing second. "Don't you have better things to be doing than speculating on my love life. Come on Ari, let's go and get breakfast."

I turned quickly, hoping they'd think I was angry. In reality, my cheeks were burning like beacons. I couldn't believe I'd just said that to my father in front of Ari. Thankfully, Ari followed, and my cheeks felt less hot by the time we got to the breakfast room.

A breakfast of croissants, jam, and butter along with some other pastries and fruit had been left out on the circular table.

My mother was already there as were Astrid and Hayden. He was looking as glum as ever, and as he saw me walk hand-in-hand with Ari, he dropped the croissant he was munching on, threw his napkin onto the table and left the room, slamming the door behind him.

"Whatever is the matter with him this morning?" my mother scrunched up her eyes.

"He's in a bad mood," I offered.

"Plainly. I just wish he'd be quieter about it," she replied, massaging her temples. "My head is still a little delicate."

She chopped her apple into slices. She always cut her food that way and ate it in tiny dainty pieces. I just gobbled things down whole. "Did you see your father?" she asked.

"Ari was with him," I replied, taking a seat and grabbing a plate. My mother raised her eyebrows at this piece of news. "He doesn't know where Ari is from, don't panic."

"I don't panic, dear; you know that," she replied, grabbing another apple.

She was obviously pretending the last couple of weeks where panic had been the constant state, hadn't happened.

"They want to go to war against the sea witch," I announced.

"Which they can't do," said Ari, picking up a croissant and dipping it in the jam.

"You don't eat croissants that way," I said, taking it from him and slicing it in two. I used a knife to take all the jam from the outside and spread it on the inside before passing it back to him. "What do you mean they can't go to war on the sea witch? We need to get the sea back."

"How? Their boats are all stuck on land now?"

"I don't know. Father and Hayden's dad are figuring it out. Some of our ships might still be at sea. Maybe he could call them all to dry land?"

My mother and Astrid watched us talking, only hearing my half of the conversation. It must have looked very funny to them.

"Havfrue is on the very horizon. The king of Havfrue will be livid that the sea witch has done this. He'll be expecting the land dwellers to be walking right out to his border. Treasure hunters, perhaps. There's no way he's going to let your father and his ships invade. The entire kingdom of Havfrue will be ready for an attack. The king hates humans. Ever since Delilah...your mother left, he's been waiting for an excuse to attack. I think this might be it."

He munched on his croissant happily as though he'd not just told me the place where he came from was gearing up for war.

"It's hardly our fault that the sea witch took the sea. Why doesn't he attack her?"

I saw my mother's eyes widen at the use of the word attack. Beside her, Astrid was staring off into space, looking miserable. Because of

Hayden, no doubt. I ignored them both and concentrated on Ari. The sea witch was our most pressing problem.

"The sea witch has been around for centuries. She's practically immortal thanks to her ability to swap and change body parts. It's part of her magic, but she has more."

"I thought my grandfather was the ultimate ruler? Doesn't he have magic?" I spoke through my mind, not wanting to mention my mother's father in front of her.

"He does, but he can't just go around murdering people for no reason. She is very influential in Havfrue."

"No reason!" I shouted out, forgetting we were talking in our heads. "She took your voice! She tried to take my legs!"

"I know that, and you know that, but the king doesn't. Anyone who has tried going up against the sea witch has either disappeared, died, or been too scared to come forward. Just as it is up here in Trifork, Havfrue has a legal system. She would have to be found guilty of her crimes, and that can take years. Despite everything she has done, a lot of people support her. She not only takes body parts for herself, she gives them to people. The ones with the most influence she doesn't ask for anything back, so a lot of people think she's great."

"What do you suggest? We let the sea stay out where it is?" I argued back. I wanted to sound strong, but arguing in your head kinda takes that away from you.

I stood up, leaving my food, and ran up to my room, feeling determined. What with the king of Havfrue planning to attack us, my father and Henry Harrington-Blythe planning goodness knows what, and Hayden being the way he was, I didn't trust anyone but myself to sort out this mess. I opened my closet door and looked at my clothes. I needed something serviceable if I was planning to walk all that way across seaweed and sand. I'd also need a good pair of shoes.

I pulled off my pajamas, jumped into some fresh underwear, and grabbed a handful of my clothes, dragging them down from their hangers.

I was in the middle of throwing them all over my bed when I heard a knock on the door. Without waiting for an answer, Ari walked in.

"So, this is how princesses live? Kinda messy," he grinned, nodding at the giant pile of ball gowns on my bed. I picked one up quickly to cover myself. I could feel the blush rising throughout my body, up past my breasts to my face where it blossomed.

"I'm going to see my grandfather," I said aloud, more to hide the color of my cheeks and my obvious embarrassment.

Ari looked at me with a stunned expression. *"You can't! A land dweller won't get in to see him. He'd never allow it. He'd kill you first."*

"Not if I was with you," I maintained.

"He'd kill me as well. He doesn't know me. I'm no one special. I'm just one of his subjects. It was dangerous just bringing you to my house on the outskirts of Havfrue last time."

"Why did you then?" I looked at him and waited for an answer.

He hesitated for a moment before speaking. *"I wanted to take you home. I wanted to pretend we could be together. I didn't care about the danger. It was worth it to have you with me."*

His words were sweet, but they didn't sway me. *"What's changed? Why can't we go now?"*

"Nothing has changed about me wanting to be with you. Last time, we sneaked into my home. This time, you are planning on going right up to the front door of the Havfrue Palace and asking to be let in."

He took my hands in his. I quivered slightly as the ball gown I was holding up in front of me fell to the floor between us, but I kept his gaze.

241

"I'm sorry, Ari, but I have to do this. I'll do it with you or without you."

He sank onto the bed, looking defeated.

I sat beside him, taking his hand. "I appreciate that this will make it hard for you, but I can't leave things like this. Just say my father does find a way to get to Havfrue? What do you think he'll do? He'll cannon the place to the ground that's what."

"I won't let you go alone," he said, picking up a sweater from underneath the mess and handing it to me. "If you really think this is the only way, I'll come with you."

"Even though it will be dangerous?"

"That's exactly why I'm coming with you," he replied squeezing my hand.

I looked into those eyes of his. They showed much more purple when he had high emotions.

"Thank you," I whispered.

He leaned forward and kissed me, making my heart pound. He'd kissed me before, but this was different. For a start, we were both in my bedroom, and I was half naked.

He brushed my hair back from my face. The touch of his hand sent my pulse soaring as he continued to run his hand through my hair and then down my spine, hitting every bump along the way, giving me goosebumps. It felt like the air was being sucked out of the room as my world was reduced to nothing but the feel of Ari's lips upon mine, the heat between us, and a moment in time I hoped would last forever. It felt so right, so perfect, and yet, I couldn't get everything going on around me out of my head. He dipped to my neck, kissing places I'd never been kissed and as the heat rose within me, I forgot all about the king of Havfrue and the sea witch that could swap and change body parts as if she was a children's toy. I forgot everything.

Havfrue

"What are you two doing in there?" called Astrid from outside of my room after giving a couple of brief knuckle raps on the door.

"Nothing," I called back, untangling myself from Ari and trying to get my breathing under control. I picked up the sweater and pulled it over my head quickly. In the closet I found a pair of trousers and some boots and tried pulling them on before answering the door, one foot in one boot, the other still on the floor when she let herself in.

She arched an eyebrow. "It sure didn't sound like nothing," she grinned. Her disappointment over Hayden's mood seemed to have subsided, thankfully. Whatever was wrong with him, it wasn't Astrid's fault. I'd already seen her two times today, but now that she was standing right in front of me, the state of her hair was worse than ever. Some of it had already begun to fall out in patches, leaving bald spots between the clumps of messy green hair. If it was worrying her, she wasn't showing it. That was Astrid all over. She took the rough with the smooth.

"We were just planning on how we were going to go visit the king of Havfrue," I said, trying not to stare too much at her hair.

Her eyes widened in surprise. "You are going to see the underwater king? Your mother is going to blow a gasket if she finds out you are planning another trip to the ocean. Are you trying to kill her off?"

I sighed, feeling bad. I'd already put my mother through so much, but what else could I do? Sit back and watch while my father and my grandfather blew each other to smithereens. "I don't feel like I have much choice. Will you help us? Can you tell her that I'm in bed with a migraine or something?" I hopped on one foot as I pulled on my other boot.

Astrid shook her head as if what I was asking of her was wrong, but she agreed anyway. "I'm going to see if Hayden wants to go out for a walk. I guess we should talk about what happened at the wedding. He's been acting weird ever since it happened."

Her cheerful demeanor dropped at the mention of Hayden, and I couldn't blame her. He was being an ass.

"What did happen at the wedding?" I asked cautiously, not at all sure I wanted to know. She seemed unusually glum about it.

"I didn't want to say anything, especially to you, but Hayden's been acting so weird ever since. He barely talks to me, and he's in such a foul mood. I think he might be disappointed that it wasn't you under the veil after all.

I broke out laughing until I saw that she wasn't joking. "You're not serious, right? Hayden doesn't want me. Maybe he was just disappointed that the wedding was cut short."

"You think?" She perked up a little at my words.

"Of course," I answered, opening the door for her. Once she left, I let out a sigh.

The truth was I wasn't sure what was going through Hayden's mind at the wedding. One thing I was pretty certain of, though, was that not marrying me was the best thing that ever happened to him. I thought back to the conversation I'd had with him the night before. He'd been acting so weird. Could Astrid be right, and he really did have feelings for me? It would explain why he was mad about the canceled wedding. It would also explain why he had such an aversion to Ari. It was nothing to do with Ari being a merman. It was because he was with me.

Surely, that couldn't be right. We'd been friends for forever. Maybe with everything that was going on at the moment, we were all a little crazy

I tried to put it to the back of my mind. I had more pressing matters to deal with. Whatever Hayden's problem was, I'd have to deal with it later.

Ari and I headed back downstairs, bypassing the breakfast room completely, and rushed outside to the gardens.

I'd escaped from the palace this way once, and if the ladder was still there, I'd be able to do it again. Amazingly, it was still propped against the wall where I'd left it. Ari let me go first, following quickly behind me. From there, getting to the edge of the sea was pretty easy. Ari took my hand as we walked along the clifftop away from the palace. If anyone spotted us, we'd look like any other pair of young lovers out for a stroll.

About a mile later, we came upon some stairs cut into the cliff face. I knew they were here despite never having used them. I'd made this walk plenty of times with various nannies.

Ari insisted on walking down in front of me so that he could catch me if I stumbled. It was sweet of him, but now that I was walking behind him, I could see how much pain he was in. He made no sound, but he trod lightly, almost limping with each step. I wondered whether he'd cry out with the agony of it if he still had his voice.

At the bottom of the stairs, we came to a beach. Usually a small beach, now it was huge with no sea surrounding it. The sea was so far away, it was barely a tiny strip of blue on the horizon. In the distance to my left, the main public beach was full of curious people, fascinated with the phenomenon. The local police and palace guards were doing a good job of stopping them from walking out too far, thankfully. I only hoped we could get out far enough before we were spotted and chased.

The walk was difficult with legs that worked. I could only imagine how awful it must be with legs that were new and painful. I gripped Ari's hand hard, letting him squeeze me when the pain became too unbearable for him.

I liked holding his hand. It wasn't passionate like it had been in the bedroom before Astrid interrupted us, but it felt natural and safe, the way my hand fit so perfectly in his. It was beyond the most wonderful feeling in the world.

Below our feet, we stepped over long green and brown strands of seaweed and mollusks in rock pools that would normally have been completely underwater. Dead fish and other ocean animals littered the sand. The sea must have gone out so quickly that they didn't stand a chance. Ari's eyes remained focused ahead, but I could see he was finding this hard. These weren't just creatures to him; they were his friends, his family. With each step, I prayed that we wouldn't see an octopus. With any luck, Ollie had been pulled out with the tide. Either that or he was still in the underwater cave. I glanced around to see if I could see it, but it wasn't apparent where it was. Maybe it was further out than the current tideline.

"How close are we to the sea witch's lair? I asked, checking out the ocean to my left."

Ari squeezed my hand more tightly. *"It's not that far from here."* He pointed to a spot in the ocean that was way too close for comfort. *"We are closer to Havfrue, though. We'll be safe there. She visits the town, but there is no way she'd dare perform any magic under the king's nose."*

"She took the tide out under the king's nose," I reminded him.

He shrugged his shoulders. *"Havfrue is still under water."*

As we got closer to the water, I wondered what my grandfather was like and whether he'd know who I was. Would he recognize me as his granddaughter? I had the same red hair as my mother, but I took my looks more after my father's side of the family.

When we were at the water's edge, Ari stripped off quickly and leaped into the waves. The look of relief on his face was evident as he swam up to the surface.

His mood and demeanor changed perceptively as he dipped in and out of the water, waiting for me to pull my boots off. I took off my trousers and sweater, folding them nicely, placing them on the sand next to me, and stepped into the water. It occurred to me that I was going to meet my grandfather, the king, no less, in my underwear. I should have thought this through a bit better, but it was too late to go back now.

"Are you going to tell him who you are?" asked Ari, pulling me along with him through the water.

I thought about it. Maybe it would make things easier, but it would also give up my mother who had spent twenty years hiding from him. *"No. I don't think so. I'll tell him I'm a friend of yours."*

Ari stopped so suddenly that I crashed right into him.

He turned and looked right at me. *"Knowing a merperson won't make a difference. The King doesn't know who I am. If anything, me bringing you to him will make things worse for both of us. He will not take this well. I know you have high hopes, but he hates land dwellers. He probably won't hurt you, but he won't be happy about you coming to Havfrue. I suspect he'll also have a few choice words for me too."*

"I'm sure we will be fine," I replied, not sure of anything at all.

I was beginning to feel more at home underwater. As Ari pulled me along, I marveled at the feel of the water rushing past my face, the feel of the warmth of the sun's rays penetrating the surface as we dashed through the coral streets of Havfrue toward the large pointed building at the far end of the vast underwater city.

It was here that Ari brought me. I didn't have to ask to know it was the royal palace. Although not as refined as the palace I was brought up in, in Trifork, it certainly equaled it for size. Four uneven turrets stood at each corner. But unlike any castle or palace I'd ever seen, the center rose up, dwarfing the towers and ended in a point just ten feet or so below the surface of the water. There were no stairs. People didn't walk here, so Ari pulled me in through a large opening that I supposed was the front door.

Two sturdily built mermen swam quickly over to us and opened their mouths to speak. One had long pale blue hair that rippled out behind him in the water and huge chest muscles that must have taken a lot of working out to acquire. The second was no less bulky, but his hair was slightly shorter, falling just past his shoulders and was the same shade as a ripe banana. When they did speak, the noise that came out of their mouths was not words, or at least, no words I could understand. It sounded like just noise. Small bubbles rose to the surface as they spoke.

Ari answered them in the same way.

One of the mermen, the yellow-haired fellow, turned on his tail and swam deeper into the palace.

"You can talk!" I exclaimed, even though I wasn't sure that's exactly what he was doing.

"Only down here. The sea witch knew what she was doing. She wanted to hurt me. Taking my underwater voice wouldn't hurt me."

"How would it not hurt you?" I asked him, trying to understand.

"I worded that wrong. It would hurt me, but not as much as not being able to talk to you. I guess she didn't expect me to have the bond with you or she would have taken my underwater voice too. In case you were wondering, I requested an audience with the king. Normally, I wouldn't have a hope of getting to see him, but I knew that bringing a human down here would give me a fast track pass to the royal room."

Seconds later, the blonde man returned and gestured us toward a corridor. My heart pounded as we swam. The corridor became smaller and smaller until we were swimming through no more than a tunnel. At first, I thought a trick was being played on us, and we'd end up coming to a dead end. But then, it opened out into the most beautiful room I'd ever seen in my life.

It reminded me of an aquarium my parents had taken me to as a child. I'd begged my mother and father to be able to go out onto the sea so many times, that they'd finally taken me to Trifork's biggest aquarium as a compromise. It was the only time I'd seen my mother around sea creatures and not be scared. Knowing what I knew now, it was because she felt at home there, and the sea witch couldn't get her. The biggest attraction at the aquarium was a long glass tunnel that wound through the actual tank, so it felt like you were underwater without having to get wet. I was mesmerized by how perfect everything looked. That is what this room looked like. The sand covering the floor was pristine, the coral decorating the walls, a perfect pink color, and the fish that swam through it were the most beautiful kinds such as neon blue angelfish, orange and black striped clownfish, and beautiful purple fish with fanlike tails. It was as if it had been curated that way. I looked up to see that we were in the very center of the palace, the part that ended up in a point. Small windows let in shafts of light and at the very top was a cage. Inside the cage, which took up about two-thirds of the space in this grand hall was a shark, a massive white shark about four times the length of me with a huge set of monstrous looking teeth. Ari shook my hand violently to bring my attention back from the terrifying shark above us. There in front of us was a sight so much worse, a sight that chilled me to my core. It was my grandfather, and boy, did he look mad.

The King

My grandfather's voice boomed out, echoing off the walls and sending the shark above into a tizzy. Long, white hair fanned out behind him, and his long, silver-white beard was tied at the front with a gold cord, stopping it from floating up in front of his face. His tail was bright green, much brighter than any of the other merpeople's tails and had a luminescence about it that was right at home in this beautiful room. I wondered for a second if my mother's tail was the same color before she lost it to the sea witch. I had no idea what he was saying, so I followed what would be protocol in my own palace and bowed deeply to him.

His laugh was not something that needed a translator. It was so loud, the walls around us shook. All I could think was that if he laughed any harder, the shark's cage was going to fall down.

"The land dweller bows at my feet," he said. I could understand him now, but his voice sounded strange underwater. He was speaking in my language for my benefit, although why my bowing down to him would be considered funny was anyone's guess.

"I'm guessing you are here because you want my help. It doesn't surprise me that the king of Trifork would send a young girl to do his dirty work, but I consider it exceptionally disrespectful of him not to come himself. Land dwellers are trash, and so, my girl, are you."

Anger bubbled up within me. Who did he think he was? I'd not opened my mouth to speak to him, and he'd already pegged me as trash. It took everything I had not to swim right up to him and tell him exactly who he was calling trash. The heir to the throne of Trifork and more importantly, the heir to the throne here. Ok, it wasn't just moral indignance that stopped me. The fact I could barely swim, and the knowledge that if I let go of Ari's hand, I wouldn't be able to breathe underwater were also contributing factors.

Ari spoke to him in their weird language. I couldn't understand a word of what they were saying, but I could tell by the way the king spoke, that it wasn't going well.

"What's going on?" I asked, panicking, but Ari didn't answer. He was too busy arguing with the king.

After what seemed like an eternity, Ari began to tug at my hand.

"Where are we going?" I asked, using all the force I could muster to pull against him. It was no use, he was so much stronger than me, and my swimming ability was practically nonexistent, to say the least. *"Stop!"*

"We can't stop, not unless you want to be that shark's lunch."

"You're joking, right?" I asked, letting him pull me now.

"Do you want to hang around to find out?"

We swam quickly through the tunnel back to the entrance of the palace, and as we exited the main door, three women swam past us. Three gorgeous women with vibrant green tails and hair the exact shade as my own. Without a doubt, these were some of my mother's sisters, but Ari didn't stop, not even for a second. He must have really believed the threat my grandfather issued. He didn't stop until we were at the water's edge. I pulled myself out and dried myself off the best I could on the sweater I'd left there, before pulling it over my head.

The way my grandfather had treated us went around and round in my head as Ari did a few flips in the water before he too pulled himself back onto the land.

I knew it was going to happen before it did, but I still wasn't prepared for the sickening sounds Ari's body made as his tail turned into legs. Nor could I get over the horrifying expression of pain on his face. When he was completely changed, he lay panting on the wet sand.

Turning from human to merman and back again was going to end up killing him.

As gently as I could, I wiped the excess moisture from his legs, dabbing them rather than rubbing, but with each touch, no matter how delicate, he cried out in pain. His skin looked angry and sore, like someone had rubbed sandpaper all over it, and as he turned to take the trousers from my hand, I could see the agony etched into every line on his face.

The walk back to the palace was a slow one. Although much stronger and faster than me underwater, Ari was walking much slower here on land. He didn't say anything, but I could tell that it was much worse for him now than it had been previously. I was almost having to pull him along in the sand to get him to move at all.

The beach was so crowded with people now, that it was inevitable that someone would spot us. My red hair was hardly discrete, and so it was the palace guards who ran out to meet us. As soon as I let go of Ari, he collapsed onto the sand.

With help from the guards, we managed to get Ari back to the palace.

My father was waiting for me in the grand hall.

"There you are!" he said, looking excited. "What's the matter with him?"

I turned to the guards holding Ari. "Please take him to the infirmary and get the nurse to look at his legs."

Ari was in too much pain to protest. I wasn't even sure he heard me through it.

"Actually, it was that chap of yours I wanted to speak to," my father cut in. "He seemed so knowledgeable about the mermaid city that I thought I'd ask him some questions."

I watched the guards carrying Ari away. It felt like part of my heart was going with him. "Not tonight, father," I mumbled. "He's not well. Maybe he'll feel well enough to help you in the morning."

"Oh, damn shame. Henry has managed to call in some of our ships that were already out at sea when the tide went out. We are going to strike tomorrow. I was hoping he'd have some advice."

My mouth dropped open in shock, but before I had time to say anything, Henry came out of the conference room and pulled my father away.

I wandered down to the infirmary, my head reeling. I'd had a bad experience in Havfrue, but that didn't mean I wanted it destroyed. Ari had mentioned that they were ready if we attacked, so did that mean they would attack back?

It didn't bear thinking about and all this because of a twenty-year-old grudge from an old crone who just happened to know magic.

Ari was barely conscious when I got to the infirmary. He was lying on a bed with his legs exposed. They looked even worse than they had at the beach. They were scaly and covered in some kind of cream.

"The nurse put it on," he said sleepily when he saw what I was looking at. *"It's supposed to help burns. I told her I hadn't been burned, but she didn't know what else to do."*

I looked around the room to see if Lucy was around. I didn't want her overhearing what I had to say next. It was only after I'd made sure that she was completely gone that I realized that she wouldn't hear us anyway.

I sighed and lowered my head until it came to a rest on Ari's chest. He ran his hand through my hair lightly, giving me goosebumps.

"Has the cream helped?" I asked, gazing down at his legs. They still looked so sore. I wasn't surprised the nurse thought he was burned.

"Not really, but the pills she gave me to sleep are doing a great job."

I sat up and looked down at his face. He was wearing a sloppy grin and looked almost drunk. His eyelids were drooping.

"My father is planning to destroy Havfrue tomorrow morning," I said to him. *"They've brought in some of our ships."*

Ari giggled. *"Have they really."*

I nodded, knowing that none of this was sinking in. Whatever the nurse had given to him was strong stuff. He closed his eyes. I waited for him to reopen them, but he was already asleep.

I really hoped the cream on his legs would help, but I doubted it. They looked like they were dying. Thinking of the sea witch and how unfair she was, I thought maybe they were.

With a heavy heart, I left the hospital wing and headed slowly upstairs to my room. I was so tired, but everything was buzzing around in my brain. Ari was hurt, his home would soon be destroyed, and he was completely out of it in the infirmary.

I'd just reached my bedroom door when my mother apprehended me.

"I'm not even going to get angry," my mother said evenly. I turned to her and tried to keep focus. She sounded resigned to everything now. She'd hidden from this mess for over twenty years and now that it had all caught up with her, she'd completely given up. "Just tell me this. Did my father mention me?"

"I didn't tell him who I was," I replied. "I didn't think you'd want me to."

I waited for her to tell me she hadn't wanted me to go to see him in the first place, but she didn't. She nodded her head and then pulled me into a hug.

"You are going to be the death of me, you know that?"

"I'm sorry, mama." I was, but I knew it was an empty apology. What I'd done today was bad, but after hearing what my father was about to do, not to mention the pain that Ari was in, I was planning something so much worse.

Sacrifice

Any plans I was formulating on how to deal with the situation had to be put on hold as Hayden barreled through my door just minutes after my mother had left.

"What do you think you are doing?" I demanded. "This is my room. You can't just walk in here."

"Why not? I've never had to wait for an invitation in the past."

The way he spoke, his lips pulled back in a sneer, I could tell he was angry.

"Because things were different then."

They were too. All the times that Hayden had been in my room, and there had been many, were innocent. Just a couple of friends hanging out together. Just as recently as a couple of weeks ago, I wouldn't have questioned Hayden walking into my room without asking. Now it seemed wrong somehow.

He sat on the bed, just as he had always done, and picked up the unicorn Ari had been picking at. "Why are they different, Erica?" His voice was full of venom. No wonder Astrid was feeling miserable if Hayden was behaving the same way with her too.

"They just are," I answered lamely. Things had changed because of Ari, and we both knew it.

"They just are," Hayden repeated back slowly. I watched as he began to pull the stitching from the unicorn. It wasn't deliberate; it was almost as though he was doing it in a trance. The poor unicorn wasn't going to survive the week with all the stress people were feeling.

"What is this all about, Hayden? Why are you so angry all of a sudden?"

He stopped picking at the stitches and looked up at me. "Don't you know? How is it possible that we have been friends for so long, and you don't know the first damn thing about me?"

"No, I don't know. You've been acting like an ass for days. Poor Astrid is upset, and you won't tell either of us what the matter is."

He stood up, throwing the unicorn onto the bed. He strode over to me and grabbed my shoulders forcefully. I sucked in my breath quickly, thinking he was going to hit me, but he drew me in towards him and kissed me violently, crushing my lips with his. Before I had any time to react, he turned around and marched out of the door leaving me alone and shell-shocked.

It took me a good few minutes to get my breathing back to its regular pace and try to comprehend what just happened.

I ran to my door and looked out. Hayden was nowhere to be seen. Without bothering to put any shoes on, I dashed down the corridor and down the stairs. I caught up with him arguing with the guard at the doorway to the balcony outside.

"Please let us through," I said to the guard sweetly. "I promise we won't go far."

The guard gave me an odd look, but he let the pair of us pass. Hayden stomped out onto the balcony and down the stairs to the promenade. He was like a small boy having a temper tantrum.

"Hayden, wait." I tried to keep up with him, my bare feet cold on the paved surface.

He turned to me, his face as dark as thunder.

"I'm going with my father tomorrow. He is riding a few miles up the coast to where the sea is unaffected, and there, he'll meet his ships.

Then, we will rid Trifork of those abominations."

Inside, I was seething. Who was he to call Ari and his kind abominations?

"Up until a few days ago, you didn't even know that merpeople existed."

"Well, I do now," he huffed.

I glared at him, unable to comprehend where all this was coming from. Hayden was usually the most inclusive person I knew. I hated the words I knew were about to come out of my mouth, but I shouted them anyway. "You are doing this because of Ari. This has nothing to do with anyone else. You are jealous of him. I just don't understand why. What has happened that you suddenly care who I'm with?"

"How could you possibly choose someone like him over me?" He shot back. "He's not even human for goodness sake."

I tried keeping my voice low and even. I didn't want everyone overhearing this conversation, not my half anyway. I was pretty sure the people in the next kingdom could hear Hayden. "I didn't choose anyone over you. You've never shown any interest in me. You've been dating Astrid for months. I thought you were happy with her. You certainly seemed like it. You never shut up about her."

He sighed and sucked in his breath as though I was being deliberately stupid.

"How can you say I've never shown any interest in you? I spent every day with you. Every single day for years!"

"We were friends," I countered, beginning to feel angry myself now. My lips felt bruised where he had kissed them.

"Friends?" he laughed, though it wasn't a laugh of mirth. He sat on the low wall, his back to the rocks and the sand.

I walked over to where he was sitting and sat beside him, not quite daring to sit too closely for fear of how he'd take it.

"Yes, friends. How was I supposed to know that you liked me in that way? You never said anything."

"I kissed you."

I wracked my brains to the last time he'd kissed me. "That was in fifth grade. We were children."

He hung his head low.

"What about Astrid?" I asked him.

"I only dated her, so you'd be jealous. I acted all happy around you, so you'd want me."

"I was happy for you both. I thought you were too."

"Well, that's just great. You were happy for us both."

He looked so lost and yet so angry. I'd never seen him like this before. I wanted to rant and rave at him. It was hardly my fault that he'd not worked up the courage to tell me how he felt. We'd known each other for years, and his proclamation of us spending every day together, while not exactly true, wasn't that far off the mark. We did spend an inordinate amount of time together.

Instead of shouting I placed my hand on his. "I'm sorry. Maybe if you'd have told me sooner, things would have been different, but the truth is, you have Astrid, and she really loves you."

"And you are dating a sea monster."

I chose to let that one slide. "I'm dating Ari, yes."

I waited for Hayden to speak, but he didn't. He kept his eyes straight down at the ground.

"What can I do?" I asked gently.

"You can leave him. Leave him and stop this thing."

I wondered if by *this thing*, he meant the war between the kings of Havfrue and Trifork.

My thoughts turned to what Ari had told me about the two of us being bonded. I couldn't leave him if I wanted to, and I really didn't want to. To pretend otherwise, even to stop a war, would be unfair to Hayden.

"I can't do that Hayden. I'm sorry. I love him."

Almost immediately, I knew it was the wrong thing to say. He ripped his hand from mine and stood up.

"Well, I hope you had the chance to say goodbye to him because after tomorrow, he won't exist anymore. My father will see to it." He stormed off leaving me alone once again. I guess no one had told him that Ari was in the hospital wing in the palace, not that it mattered. Hayden and his father were still going to either kill or be killed tomorrow. It only made me more determined to set out to put my plan into action tonight. First, I needed to get changed. I headed back up the stairs quickly. Just as I was about to head back into the palace, I caught the outline of someone in the shadows. Someone who didn't want to be seen. They were weeping softly. I could have imagined it, but I was sure I saw a hint of green hair.

After everything that had happened with Hayden, once I got changed, I headed down to the infirmary. I needed to see Ari, even though I knew he'd be sleeping. I needed his presence beside me as I decompressed from the massive fall out with Hayden. I stayed for a few hours, watching him sleep, the rise and fall of his chest beneath the covers. In the short space of the time that I'd known him, he'd become everything to me. No one, not even Hayden, would spend his life in pain just to be with me. I wouldn't want him to either, just like I didn't want Ari to. Enough was enough. Too many lives had been impacted by the sea witch's actions already, and even though my grandfather treated me like dirt when I went to warn him, tomorrow the whole of Havfrue would be blown to smithereens if I didn't do something quickly.

Just after midnight, I slipped away from the infirmary, gently kissing Ari's cheek before I left. He didn't stir. I slipped off my mother's necklace, the ruby of Havfrue and left it on his bedside table. I knew it was the only thing I had to keep me safe from the witch but keeping safe wasn't my main agenda. Whatever drugs the nurse had administered to Ari had sent him into a deep sleep which was just as well. I didn't want him waking and trying to stop me.

There were more guards than I thought there would be on the shorefront, but it was a cloudy night, and the moon kept disappearing behind them, pitching us all into darkness. I just had to wait until one of the clouds hovered in front of the moon before making a dash for it. I ran as fast as my feet would carry me, doing my best to dodge rocks and slippery seaweed. Ari had pointed out where the sea witch lived, to the left of Havfrue. I didn't need to worry about swimming to her, I only had to dip my toes in the ocean near her cave, to have her come to find me. The water sounded so gentle as tiny waves lapped at my feet, that it was almost impossible to imagine the horror of what I was about to face.

At the sea line, I strode purposefully into the ocean, waiting for the blackness to appear. I wouldn't see it. It was so dark out that all the ocean looked black, but I knew she would come, and when she did, I'd be able to breathe underwater. At least, that's what I told myself as I allowed my body to slip below the briny surface.

It didn't take long. Less than twenty seconds after submerging myself, I felt the strong current pulling me away from the shore. Another few seconds, and I was breathing quite normally under the water. A tentacle wrapped itself around my arm, terrifying me as it pulled me through the water. This was no octopus, though. This was the sea witch.

Her cave looked the same as it had the last time I'd been there, but this time, I knew I wasn't going to escape. I'd already decided that tonight was the night I was going to die, and I'd made my peace with it.

The greenish purple walls looked even more eerie, knowing that this was to be my final resting place.

"I didn't expect you to come here again," the sea witch eyed me up as she let go of my arm. Her eyes darted down to where the necklace had been around my neck, and I noticed she kept her distance.

"I'm not here to hurt you. I'm here to surrender myself. This is what it's always been about. Right from the very start, you wanted me. Well, now you have me." I made a step toward her, but she kicked off the ground using her tentacles and floated backward, kicking up some sand as she did.

Her brows drew together. "Why?" she asked, keeping a safe distance from me. Her hair, or should I say Astrid's hair floated about her, the only beautiful part she had. I wondered what part of me she'd steal. Maybe all of me. I pushed the thought to the back of my head.

"I'll give myself to you on a couple of conditions," I announced keeping still so as not to shock her.

She arched a brow. "What conditions?"

"Firstly, I'm here in payment for my mother's legs. She promised you her firstborn, and here I am. Now that you have me, I want you to stay clear of Trifork and any of my family. I want my

272

brother to be able to swim freely in the ocean in a way that I never was."

"Some would say that would be a fair swap and no other conditions should be attached," she mused aloud.

"Maybe, but you've hurt a lot of people, and even though I haven't known you to play fair, I think you believe that one exchange deserves another. You took Astrid's hair without giving her anything in return. By your own rules, you owe her something."

I had no idea if this was true. She'd certainly demanded something back from my mother and had swapped with Ari – his voice for his legs. I had a feeling that there was an interest in fairness within her somewhere.

I could feel my heart beating rapidly beneath my breast. Issuing demands to a sea witch was one of the hardest things I'd ever had to do. But knowing that I was planning on ending my life here, being strong and standing my ground was easier than I expected it to be.

"Secondly, I want you to put the water back. The people of Havfrue and the people of Trifork have not wronged you. If you leave the water out, they are planning on war. I don't want anyone else being hurt. You have to leave the city of Havfrue alone. You've caused enough damage there."

She nodded.

"Finally, I want you to stop the pain in Ari's legs and give him his voice back."

"You are asking a lot, young lady. What makes you think that you are worth it?"

I'd been thinking about it a lot ever since she'd been scared by the necklace. My grandfather was a powerful man—the most powerful man in the ocean. When his eldest daughter came to her all those years ago, it must have been a dream come true for the witch. A young woman full of the power of the ocean, willing to give her anything she wanted in exchange for legs. She could have taken anything, but knowing that she would live a long time, to get someone even younger with the same royal power, she had decided to wait for the princess to have a baby. A baby, she could watch grow and feed off her power. When the time was right, she'd steal her body parts and use them for her own. Then, and only then, she would be equal to the king.

"You cannot beat the king without me. I know you've tried. You might have been able to do it with my mother, but your magic doesn't work like that. You can't take without giving. Well, you gave my mother her legs; you can take me without consequences."

Of course, there would be consequences, but not to her magic. I knew what I was doing would risk the town of Havfrue. If she used me to become all powerful and try to take over, I'd only be swapping one problem for the king for another.

What the sea witch didn't know was that I had no powers. She'd seen me with the necklace and believed it was me that controlled it. But the truth of the matter was, the necklace was powerful without my help. I hadn't done anything the last time I'd been here. The necklace had worked all on its own. By the time the witch figured that out, the water would be back to where it should be, and Ari would no longer be in pain. At least, that was the plan.

The sea witch nodded her head again as she circled around me. The weird water in her cave seemed to have no effect on her as she swam through it, keeping an eye on me.

"Ok," she said, accepting my offer. "You ask a lot of me, but you are right. I've taken without giving, and that is unacceptable to me. I will do everything that you ask, but first, you must remove that necklace."

I pulled my shirt down slightly to show her that I was no longer wearing it. "I left it back at the palace."

The way she looked at me sent shivers down my spine. Her eyes crinkled up at the edges in glee as she realized I was completely helpless against her.

She waved her hands about, disturbing the water around her, sending ripples through it that tickled my cheeks. I felt the magic force all around me, but I had no way of knowing just what magic she'd done.

"I've done everything you asked," she said once the magical disturbance died down. "Now, come to me."

"I need to see it for myself first," I demanded.

She wrapped a tentacle around my arm and pulled me up through the hole in the ceiling to the surface. Even with the night being as dark as it was, it was easy to see the reflections in the water of the palace lights, and of the other buildings that were dotted along the shorefront.

"There you have it," she said, a tone of amusement in her voice. "The sea is back to normal. Your boyfriend is the same. He'll be pain-free by tomorrow morning. I have also given him his voice back. I believe that's everything you asked. More than you asked for even."

I nodded. I'd saved my family. I'd saved Ari. The people of Havfrue would still have to deal with her, but she wouldn't be any more powerful than she was now, no matter what parts of me she took. In the eighteen years I'd been alive, I'd shown no promise of having any magic. I was sure to be a huge disappointment to her, and that's what I was gambling on. I closed my eyes as the witch pulled me back beneath the surface. Back inside her cave, I stood and waited for whatever she had in store for me.

The shock on her face was evident. I think she was waiting for some kind of trick that never came.

"You really came here to give yourself to me? I was expecting a fight."

I nodded slowly, suddenly feeling the enormity of what I'd done. I slowly took a step towards her, my arms outstretched in front of me.

A menacing smile erupted on her lips as I closed the gap between us.

"There is just one more piece of magic I'd like you to perform," I said, taking a step backward. What with everything else I'd asked for, I'd almost forgotten the most important bit of all. "This magic is not to rectify something you have done. It's...it's a favor to me."

She laughed, but I could see she was intrigued. I was pretty sure she'd do it for me. She had nothing to gain by not doing so.

"Ari and I are bonded. I want you to cut the bond, so he may live after I die."

I saw her thinking it through. "Why would I do that? It will benefit me in no way."

"I'm giving myself to you, all of me. You don't need Ari. You took his voice and didn't use it. You barely used any of the crew of the *Erica Rose*. You want to be beautiful."

"It's a shame," she mused taking a step toward me and running her hands through my fiery red hair. "I'd have preferred this color, but it would be such a shame to waste this beautiful blonde hair I already have. I'll take your legs, of course. Tentacles are handy for getting around the ocean, but oh, so cumbersome on land."

"On land?" I was taken aback. As far as I knew, she was unable to go on land.

Her eyelashes fluttered as she laughed at me. "Why, of course, child. With your legs and your lungs, I'll be whole again and finally able to fulfill my destiny."

My eyes narrowed as I took in her words. "What do you mean?"

"Why, you don't think I like living here in this cesspit of a cave, do you?" Her face contorted to a picture of evil amusement.

"Do you really think this place is a fitting home for someone as powerful as I?" Her cackle somehow echoed around the cavern despite it being filled with water. It really was some strange magic. "The king banished me from Havfrue years ago, and although I do still pop in from time to time, I am unable to stay long, thanks to his magic. The closest place I could find was this cave, but I deserve better than this and with my new body, I mean to get it. The king of Havfrue is, unfortunately, a much stronger opponent than I can handle in my old age, but the king of Trifork, well, he has no magic, does he? Taking over on land should be a snap."

I stared at her in horror. "You can't!"

"My dear, of course, I can. You asked me to spare Havfrue. You said nothing about Trifork. Who is going to stop me? Not your boyfriend. He will die along with you. I'm so glad you told me that the pair of you were bonded. It will make it so much easier."

I stepped back again, but this time with good reason. I'd gone to the old hag in good faith, but she had never played fair, and it didn't look like she was about to start now.

"Don't run, deary," she called mockingly. "There's nowhere to go."

With a smirk on her face, she swam up to me and grabbed me by the arm. Despite her age, her strength was exceptional. Out of nowhere, she produced a knife which she held up with her other hand right in front of my eyes so I could see it. A flash of purple ran through it. This was no ordinary knife. It contained magic.

"Now, my beautiful darling, I'll take those legs of yours. In a few minutes, you won't be needing them anymore."

The underwater palace

I screamed as she lowered the knife down to the top of my thigh. This time, though, no sound came out. The strange underwater atmosphere had changed perceptively. We were now in real water. Real water where I couldn't talk, walk normally, and most importantly, breathe.

Salt water filled my mouth as I writhed to pull myself from her grip. In my panic, I couldn't see what she was doing, but I could feel it. A sharp stinging sensation hit me as she ran the sharp blade through my trousers and across the skin of my thigh. If I could have cried out, I would have. The pain was intense, but I couldn't make any noise as I struggled to pull myself away from the knife.

I couldn't hear her speaking either, but I could see the expression on her face. It left no doubt that she was laughing manically as she tore through my flesh. Blood—my blood—clouded my vision, and I honestly thought I was going to pass out. Dizziness engulfed me, and without being able to take deep breaths to quell it, it took everything I had not to succumb to the darkness.

"*Ari!*" I shouted as loudly as I could in my mind. He was the only one who'd ever been able to hear me this way, but he was a mile away, tucked up in bed after consuming drugs to help him sleep. Even if by some amazing miracle I managed to drag him from his drug-induced slumber, there was not a chance in a million years he'd be fast enough to get to me. Not now. My time left was counting down in seconds rather than minutes, and yet, I still yelled his name. I wanted him to know that it he was the subject of my final thoughts.

The water all around me was now bright red. My own blood had clouded it so much, I couldn't even see the witch in front of me, but I could still feel her strong grip on my arm and the knife digging into my flesh.

My eyes felt heavy as unconsciousness began to creep in, brought on by a lack of oxygen. Darkness pressed down on me and I knew I should let myself succumb to it. Anything was better than the excruciating agony that now running through my leg.

I'd come here completely expecting it to be my last act ever, but it had backfired on me. In wanting to save the people of Trifork and my own family, I'd inadvertently made things so much worse for them. With every ounce of the energy left to me, I fought against her, but like a mouse fighting a lion, I had no chance of winning. The best I could hope for would be to inflict some pain as my life ended. I grabbed her hand and forced the knife backward hoping to strike her. A deathly scream told me I'd hit my mark, but it was too late to save me. I was already dying.

I blinked, ready to take my last look when there was a flash of something in front of me. The water all around us displaced quickly, and the pressure on my arm let up as the witch let go of me. Another great swish of water sent me hurtling backward and down to the seabed.

My leg felt like it was on fire, but the shock of the sudden movement had me opening my eyes widely, trying to make sense of what was going on.

Huge white teeth cut through meat in front of me sending another plume of red into the water. All I could see around me was blood. My own?

I closed my eyes, ignoring the currents of water pulsating around me and finally gave in to the darkness.

I felt movement. Either water was whooshing past me, or I was being pulled through it. I didn't have the energy to open my eyes to see which it was. I had never felt so dizzy and sick in my life, but somewhere in the back of my mind, I wondered if it was Ari who was pulling me through the ocean.

"I love you," I murmured in my mind, but I was either too out of it, or he hadn't heard me because there was no response.

I was aware I was breathing again, although I could feel that I was still underwater. I drifted in and out of consciousness, neither knowing nor caring where I was going. After a while, the feeling of being pulled through water abated, and I was laid down gently.

"Ari!" I shouted his name, but my voice sounded strange as though I was in a chamber of some kind. My throat hurt, and I could taste the salt in it. I was also aware that I was no longer underwater. The air around me was stale and smelled fishy, but at least, I was breathing again, really breathing, not aided by magic. My leg throbbed as I tried to pull myself back to full consciousness. I could definitely smell and hear, although the noises around me felt distant and strange. I could also feel and knew I wasn't in a normal bed. It felt like I was on a beach. A cold beach. There was definitely sand beneath me. But opening my eyes to see was a struggle. I felt like I was trying to claw my way out of a dark pit.

"Don't fight it. You need to heal, to sleep." I felt a damp cloth graze over my forehead. The voice was calming. Whoever had spoken was obviously taking care of me, but I didn't recognize the woman's voice. With everything that had happened to me, being incapacitated in a strange place with someone I didn't know made me feel even worse.

"Where is Ari?" I mumbled, my voice tight with the salt caking my throat. I should be asking for a drink to wash it down.

"I don't know, honey, but you've been calling for him in your sleep."

I had? I wanted to ask her who she was, where I was, but exhaustion was winning the battle. Wherever I was, I knew I was safe. Without opening my eyes, I allowed myself to drift into unconsciousness.

When I awoke, maybe hours, maybe days later, I felt so much better. My leg still hurt like hell, but opening my eyes wasn't the struggle it had been.

I found myself in the strangest room. The walls were made of the most beautiful pink coral, and the floor was a bed of pristine sand on which I was currently lying. It looked and sounded like I was underwater, but I could breathe normally. It wasn't the weird breathable water of the witch's cave, but real oxygen. And yet, I'd never seen a place like this above the water. I pulled myself into a sitting position to try and get a better look at my surroundings to work out where I was, but as I did, pain flooded through me. I gasped, looking down at my leg. Someone had bandaged it tightly, but I could still see a few spots of red where my blood had seeped through. I gritted my teeth until the pain subsided and then looked around the room again. Apart from myself, the room was empty.

"Hello," I cried out, my voice straining.

Less than a minute later, a woman walked in. Actually, she pulled herself in by her hands as she had no legs to walk on, only a breathtaking iridescent pink tail that trailed in the sand behind her.

"I'm sorry," she huffed as she pulled herself over to my side. "I'm not used to this."

She nodded down to her tail "I've always swum before. This is new."

She was stunningly beautiful with long red hair so much like my own and a face that looked eerily similar to my mothers.

"You are one of the king's daughters," I observed, recognizing her. I'd seen her in passing the last time I was here with Ari.

"Yes. My name is Adella," she smiled pleasantly pouring me a glass of water, which she handed to me. I took it and drank it down greedily, thankful I was finally able to rid myself of the salt clogging my throat. She poured me another glass which I also downed quickly.

"My father made that for you. He desalinated it."

"Desalinated?"

"He took the salt out. You land dwellers don't do well with saltwater. Can I ask you a question?"

She looked at me in a strange way. I had an idea what she was going to ask. I nodded my head.

"Are you Anaitis' daughter? You look so much like her. Your hair..."

"My hair is just like yours. I am her daughter. You must be one of her sisters."

She gave a small laugh, little more than a puff of breath. "I never thought I'd see any child of hers. I'm so glad that I have, although I would have liked to meet you under better circumstances. Are you an only child?"

I shook my head. "I have a younger brother, but he's not allowed in the ocean. My mother was always worried that the sea witch would take him...and me."

Adella took my hand and smiled widely. Tears pooled at the corners of her eyes as she spoke. "You don't need to worry about the sea witch anymore."

"She's dead?" I asked, not daring to hope it was true.

"The king has been desperate to stop the sea witch for a long time, but there are laws here. He has known for a while that she has been up to no good, but until last night, he had no proof. She preyed on the people that she knew wouldn't tell the king. That's how she's managed to keep what she's been up to under wraps for so long."

"So, my grandfather killed her?"

"He saw what the witch was going to do to you, so he set his pet on her."

I thought back to the fearsome shark in the cage above the king's head in the throne room. It certainly explained all the blood I saw. It wasn't all from my leg after all. It was the blood of the sea witch.

"I thought the king hated me," I mumbled.

"He did. He hates all land dwellers, but then something about you changed his mind."

"What?"

Her face brightened. "I saw you when you came to see him yesterday. There was something about you. Of course, you caused a sensation by just being here with legs instead of a tail. There was an uproar, but it was only after you had gone that I put two and two together.

"I went to father with my assumption about who you were. He took a lot of convincing, but then he came around to the idea that you might be his granddaughter.

"When one of the guards spotted you walking across the sand and told him, he decided to see where you went. I think he was surprised to see you heading straight toward the sea witch's cave."

"What happened?" I asked. "I don't even remember seeing him there."

"He heard what you said to her, about how you wanted Havfrue protected, along with Trifork. I think that's what finally convinced him who you were."

I had wanted Havfrue saved. It was my ancestral home, and even though I couldn't breathe underwater, I did feel at home here.

There was something missing though. I now knew it was my grandfather and not Ari who had brought me back here, but I was surprised he hadn't come looking for me.

"Where is Ari?" I asked.

Adella cocked her head to the side. "Ari? The boy you've been talking about in your sleep?"

"My boyfriend." It was the first time I'd called him that. It felt weird saying it to this stranger, but how else could I describe him?

"Is that the boy you came here with yesterday?"

I nodded

"I'm afraid I haven't seen him. There's a good chance he won't know you are here unless you told him where you were going. Even then, unless he saw the king save you, he wouldn't know where to look for you."

Everything she said made sense. Of course, Ari didn't know where I was. He had no reason to think that I'd be in the King of Havfrue's castle.

"How long will I have to stay here?" I asked, thinking that I'd go straight home and tell everyone where I was. It wasn't just Ari that would be worried. My parents would too.

"You need to rest. You got hurt pretty badly and need time to heal. The king has used his magic to provide a room of oxygen for you. In a couple of days, he will take you back to your own land himself."

"A couple of days!" I blurted, pulling myself up quickly. A slice of pain shot through me, making me whimper.

"Yes. A couple of days. We will do what we can to heal you using our healing balms, but they take time."

I lay myself back as she gently removed the bandage on my thigh. She applied some green goop which soothed my painful skin and then rebandaged it.

"Please, will you go to Trifork, to the palace and tell them that I'm alright?"

Her eyes widened as she took in what I was asking of her.

"I can't do that," she answered fearfully.

"You have to," I begged. "My family will be out looking for me. You know my parents are the king and queen. They already have half the navy called back to Trifork. They were going to use the ships to blow up Havfrue. Now, they won't, but they will use them to come looking for me. Do you really want hundreds of ships above Havfrue, because here is the first place they will look for me."

She closed her eyes, inhaling a deep breath. "You don't understand what you are asking of me."

"I'm only asking you to swim a mile and tell someone where I am. It doesn't have to be your sister. You could tell one of the guards outside the palace."

"I'll do what I can," she conceded, "But you have to rest up. That leg isn't going to heal by itself."

She finished bandaging me up and then pulled herself back through the door the way she had come. As I watched her leave, I saw a rippling effect at the doorway that I'd not noticed before. Beyond the doorway was water, only held back by magic.

I lay back and waited

The two days Adella promised me I'd be here became three, dragging on for what felt like an eternity. On the morning of the third day, Adella came to let me know that the king was on his way to see me. Since the first day, she hadn't been back. Instead, merpeople I assumed were palace servants brought me food and water. I was just about to ask her if she'd had the chance to go to my parent's palace when my grandfather came floating in behind her.

The king had such an imposing presence that I was surprised when he came into my room without making a sound. Unlike Adella who had been pulling herself into and out of the room, the king used magic, floating silently towards my makeshift bed on the sand. On seeing him, Adella bowed and left as quickly as she was able to.

"Thank you for saving me," I began, but he raised his hand to stop me.

"I've been angry for a very long time," he admitted, his voice booming, resonating around the strange underwater room. "But I came to realize with the help of Adella and my other daughters that it is not you that I'm angry with."

"My mother hates the fact that she has never been able to come home. She was terrorized by the sea witch and told that if she ever stepped foot in the ocean again, the sea witch would take her legs and her voice. She's been afraid of the water ever since. I think she wanted to come home, she just couldn't."

The old man turned his head away from me and brought his hand to his mouth as if he was crying. It was so incongruous to his fearsome persona to see him weeping. When he turned back, his eyes were dry, but the redness around the edges gave him away.

"I could ask her to come visit," I offered, "if you want her to, that is. I'm sure she would love to come home now that the sea witch is dead."

His mouth set in a hard line. "It is not just that. I have long since been wary of the land dwellers. Look how quick they were to declare war on us. She chose the land dwellers over us, and that is unacceptable."

I sat up and looked him straight in the eye. "She chose love. As her father, I would have thought you would want her to be happy."

He nodded his head slowly but didn't answer.

"I will take you back to the land. I believe you are well enough to travel now. Adella tells me that your leg is healing nicely."

I bent my leg at the knee. It still hurt, but not to the extent it had three days previously.

"Adella has done a wonderful job. Please thank her for me."

He nodded his head and then, without asking, scooped me up and carried me through the door and out into the water.

The journey back to the palace took almost no time at all, and my grandfather stopped by the small dock. One of the palace guards drew his sword and came running over to us.

"Stop!" I yelled. "It's me."

"Is this how all your people greet visitors?" asked my grandfather quietly in my ear. I was just about to answer him when my mother flew out of the house, her gray-streaked hair flying in the wind behind her.

The guard stepped back to let her through, but she didn't stop. With a leap, she dove headfirst into the water.

When she surfaced, she flung her arms around me, holding me tight. I could hear her weeping.

"I'm ok," I murmured, once again, feeling terrible. Of all the people in the world I'd have to make this up to, my mother was at the top of my list. She stroked my dripping wet hair, burying my face in her shoulder, which shook with her sobbing.

"Thank you for bringing her back," she stammered between sobs. I couldn't see my grandfather's reaction, but I assumed he nodded because she invited him inside for tea.

"It's about time I told my husband who I really am."

My grandfather and the guard helped my mother and me out of the water. My grandfather didn't need any help, He floated up using his magic, letting the ocean water drip off him. The guard's eyes widened at this huge white-bearded man with a tail floating past him.

"At least, this news is going to completely eclipse your wedding fiasco," joked my mother.

My grandfather began to laugh as I'd told him all about the wedding as we were swimming, but I had other things on my mind.

"Where is Ari?" I asked her, looking around for him. "Is he still in the hospital wing?"

"I don't know, honey. He left three days ago. Before Adella came to tell me where you were, I thought he'd gone to look for you. He never came back."

Merman lost

I raced up to the hospital wing even though my mother had just told me he'd already left.

The bed he had been in was now freshly made. On the bedside cabinet beside it my mother's necklace, the Havfrue ruby was exactly where I'd left it. It hadn't been touched at all. I picked it up and slipped it around my neck as Lucy, the nurse entered.

"You're back!" she exclaimed in delight, making a beeline straight for me and wrapping me in her arms. "Have you spoken to your mother yet? She's been beside herself with worry."

I told her I had. "What happened to Ari?" I asked, fingering the ruby around my neck. It was strange that he'd leave it there.

"I don't know. The day you disappeared, he just vanished."

"Vanished? He didn't say where he was going?"

Lucy shook her head. "I didn't see him leave for him to say anything. Before your parents came to tell me about you, Ari had already gone. His bed was empty."

If he'd left before finding out I'd gone, why had he left? Was he in so much pain that he'd gone back to the sea without saying goodbye? Then, it occurred to me that he could have come to say goodbye and found my room empty.

I thanked Lucy and dashed back outside. At the very edge of the rocks, the furthest point I could go to without getting wet, I shouted his name, both in my head and out loud. The only answer I got was the call of a couple of gulls. As I made my way back to the palace, I saw a large group of people gathering. Many of them had cameras. It looked like the press had already gotten wind of my grandfather's visit. It didn't take long for the news to spread. Ignoring them, I ran back inside the palace.

I could hear my grandfather's booming voice coming from the parlor. To my surprise, he, my mother, and my father were sitting eating scones and drinking tea.

"If I'd have known how good scones were, I'd have come up on land years ago," he laughed.

They all seemed to be getting along so well. Who knew that decades of hatred could be brought down with a few pastries and some clotted cream?

"I need help," I said breathlessly, interrupting their little party. "I need someone to take me back into the ocean to find Ari."

My father's eyebrows shot up. "Don't tell me that he's a merperson too? No wonder the lad knew a lot. What a week!"

"I'll take you," my grandfather offered.

My mother sat up in alarm. "I don't want you to go yet. You only just got here." She turned to me. "I'm sure your friend will be alright."

My grandfather stood up, or rather floated, out of his chair. "I'll come back, Anaitis. You have my word."

My mother gave me a huge smile as my grandfather came to me. I'd made it up to her. I'd made everything up to her. Bringing her father back was worth all the stress I'd caused her. At least, I hoped it was. My mother and father walked us out to the promenade. As soon as we left the palace, the photographers at the other side of the fence began snapping pictures. Both my grandfather and my father waved. Even my mother cracked a smile at the reporters. Everyone was happy it seemed but me. Something had happened to Ari. I knew it.

There was no way he'd just leave the palace. If he'd been in the water when the sea witch was hurting me, he'd have heard me crying out for him.

My trepidation intensified as I jumped back into the water. Over the past couple of weeks, I'd learned enough to tread water until my grandfather lowered himself in. He touched my hand and I was able to breathe as we both dove under the surface. Being pulled along by my grandfather was no less exciting than when Ari did it, but it was much lonelier. My grandfather couldn't hear me the way Ari could, and I couldn't speak to him. I had no way to communicate with him beyond pointing. I had such difficulty remembering where the cave was but after an hour or so, I found the entrance. The cave was dark with only a few shafts of light pouring through. Even so, it was easy to see that Ari wasn't there. He wasn't in his small underwater house in Havfrue either. My grandfather, maybe in an attempt to make it up to me, took me along every coral-lined street in Havfrue to no avail. We asked around and found a few people who knew him, but no one had seen him for days. Eventually, we had to give up and head back to land.

As we broke the surface near the dock, he turned and thanked me.

"What for?" I asked, but I already knew. I'd righted a wrong that had happened twenty years ago. I'd reunited him with his eldest daughter. He took hold of the Havfrue Ruby around my neck.

"You know, I gave this to your mother on her eighteenth birthday with the promise there was enough magic in it to grant her one wish. I cannot believe after all these years, she's not found anything important to wish for."

"What do you mean?"

He smiled and let the ruby go. "It still holds its magic. I can feel it. I guess the wish now belongs to you."

"If this holds a wish, why didn't she wish for legs instead of visiting the sea witch? It would have saved us all a lot of trouble."

He nodded. "It would. Perhaps she didn't realize just how powerful the Havfrue Ruby is...perhaps she didn't want to use anything associated with me."

I kissed his cheek as he left me on the shore with the promise he'd be back to visit soon.

I made my way up to my bedroom and flopped down on the bed. The pain in my leg was now only a dull ache, but I used it as an excuse to think about something other than Ari. My head had been full of nothing but thoughts of him for hours, wondering where he was. I poured myself a bath and pulled off the dressings that Adella had applied. My leg was almost healed. She'd done an amazing job. Whatever was in those sea herbs of hers certainly worked better than anything I'd seen used on land. A faint scar still showed, practically silver on the skin of my thigh where the sea witch had cut.

However hard I tried not to worry about him, my thoughts turned back to Ari. If he'd decided to go back to the ocean, why wasn't he at home? If he'd gone to the sea witch, he'd have found her gone. No matter how hard I tried to think of where he could be, I couldn't come up with a plausible reason for him to disappear like that.

I'd just finished shampooing my hair when I heard a knock on my bedroom door. I quickly rinsed off and wrapped a towel around myself. I should have dressed before opening the door, but somewhere in the back of my mind, I wondered if it was Ari, finally back from wherever he'd been. If I let him wait too long, he might leave again.

I opened the door quickly. It wasn't Ari. Astrid, her hair a mess of straggly green and contrasting red eyes ran past me without waiting for an invite.

I'd seen Astrid upset before, but I'd never seen her cry. She just wasn't the crying type. Snot dribbled down from her nose, and her cheeks were red and blotchy. In short, she looked a mess.

I passed her a towel and sat next to her on the bed. I'd been so caught up in my own stuff, I'd not spared a thought for Astrid. The last few weeks had been tough on her. First with the public rejection of marriage to Hayden, then losing her beautiful hair. I didn't know what had happened more recently to make her react the way she was, but I could hazard a guess.

"Is this to do with Hayden?" I ventured. She nodded.

"What has he done now?" The guy had been acting like a total ass the last time I saw him. If he'd been that way with me, I could only guess how he'd been with Astrid. He'd told me he was only dating her to get back at me.

"He proposed to me."

Of all the words I expected to come out of her mouth, never in a million years would I have guessed those.

"He asked you to marry him?"

She nodded her head and wiped her nose at the same time.

I knew I should be smiling and congratulating her, but after what he'd said to me the last time he'd seen me and the state of her now, I was rendered speechless.

"I know he loves you," she hiccupped. "I overheard you two talking the other night."

"I'm sorry," I began, not knowing what else to say.

"It's okay," she replied wistfully. "I don't blame you for anything. It was apparent that you had no idea of his feelings any more than I did." She sniffed again, so I handed her another tissue.

"You said no to him, right?"

"I said yes," she replied with a small smile on her face. It was not the happiest of smiles. "I know what you are thinking. Why would I say yes, knowing that he doesn't love me, knowing that he's in love with someone else."

"I was wondering."

"He's a good catch. His father is the admiral of the navy, and he's a sea captain. He confessed everything after I confronted him and told me he wanted a second chance."

I tried wrapping my head around what she was telling me. He only confessed to her after she told him that she'd overheard everything he'd said to me. Would he have done that if she'd not heard anything? It wasn't this that gave me pause, though. It was something else she'd said.

"What do you mean sea captain? Hayden isn't a sea captain."

She smiled again, this time a genuine smile full of happiness. I could see the pride in her face. "Actually, he is. He was offered the position a few days ago after volunteering to go out to sea and bomb Havfrue when the tide was way out. Not many men would do it, but Hayden was the first in line."

I hated him then. First in line to bomb Havfrue. It made me sick. He must have gone straight to his father after our little talk. After I'd told him that I was in love with Ari.

"When did he propose?" I asked.

"It was the morning after you disappeared, not that we knew that you'd disappeared at the time. He was on his way to his boat when I apprehended him. He didn't have much time, he was on his way to handle some important mission, but he asked me to marry him."

Just hours after declaring his love for me, he'd proposed to Astrid. What a louse!

"Do you really want to marry him, Astrid? After everything that you now know about him?"

"I do. I really do. I know it's not perfect, but I love him."

I knew how love can make you do crazy things. I was willing to give up my life for Ari, but I knew he loved me back...or at least, I thought he did. Now with him missing, I wasn't so sure. Maybe I was as naive as Astrid was. Maybe we were both lovesick idiots together. Still, some of the things she said didn't quite add up.

"If you want to marry Hayden despite everything, why are you so upset? What are the tears for?"

"He's been gone for a few days. I haven't seen him since the proposal. He told me he didn't want to marry me the way I looked. He said I looked ghastly and that I should find someone to bleach my hair back blonde. I don't know what to do. I was hoping I could somehow go to the sea witch and beg for my hair back, but I was just told that the sea witch is dead. I'm stuck with this forever." She pulled a clump of hair up and let it fall again.

I couldn't believe Hayden would say such a thing, but the fact that Astrid still agreed to marry him was even more unbelievable. Astrid was a strong woman. What had Hayden done to her to make her want him so badly that common sense flew out the window?

I desperately wanted to find Ari, but Astrid needed me more right now.

"My mother employs hairdressers. I could ask one to come up and help with your hair, but before I do that, I think we need to talk."

Astrid gave me a grateful smile. I wondered if she'd still be so happy when I finished telling her what I thought.

By the time the hairdresser arrived an hour later, Astrid had heard all I had to say. I'd always loved Hayden, but the way he was behaving right now was downright obnoxious, and I wasn't about to let Astrid get herself caught up in whatever was going on with him.

She listened. There were tears, but she took in everything I had to say. My heart almost broke for her as I spelled out what her life would be like married to someone who bossed her around and, worst of all, was only doing it to make someone else jealous.

As the hairdresser got all her equipment out and laid it neatly on the bed, Astrid took a deep breath and nodded. This past week had been tough on her, and her strength had been zapped, but I saw the look of determination on her face as she followed the hairdresser into my en-suite bathroom.

As I waited, I tried piecing together everything that she'd told me about Hayden. Not about his love for me. I already knew that. I needed to find out more about where he was. She'd told me he was in a rush when he left. He left the same day as Ari disappeared. I hated thinking it, but in the back of my mind, I wondered if Hayden had something to do with Ari's disappearance.

Whichever way I looked at it, the timing of everything seemed suspicious. The morning I was found missing was the same day that Ari also disappeared, and it was the same morning that Hayden left, supposedly on his own ship. I didn't want to believe that Hayden would do anything so awful, but the way he'd been acting recently, I wouldn't put anything past him. My heart ached at what Hayden had turned into. He claimed it was because of unrequited love for me, but even that didn't add up. Yeah, he'd kissed me once, but it was so many years ago. Surely, if he had a crush on me, I'd have noticed? I sighed, not knowing what was going on in his mind. I'd always been able to read him like a book before and now...?

"What do you think?"

Astrid stepped out of the bathroom looking amazing. The hairdresser had done something so wild, so fantastic that Astrid had never looked better. She'd not done what Hayden had asked of her. She'd done something so much better. The hairdresser had shaved the sides of

Astrid's hair, leaving it long on top. The messy algae color it was before was now a much brighter green with blue ends that fell in glossy waves down her back. The grin on Astrid's face told me that I'd done the right thing in telling her not to follow Hayden's wishes. If he loved her, he'd love her no matter what her hair color was, and I had to say, she'd never looked cooler. My parents would probably not be too happy about having a green and blue-haired, partly shaven, lady of the court. However, I could hear reporters shouting all the way up here, so I figured they had enough on their plates not to worry about hair color. One thing was for certain, the royal family was getting its fair share of airtime on the kingdom's news stations.

"You look...I can't even express how fantastic you look. I love it. It looks like you jumped off the cover of a trendy magazine."

"I know," she squealed, jumping up and down. "It's amazing. I love it too."

And with that, the Astrid I knew was back to her old self.

While she'd been getting her hair done, I'd been mulling over a theory, and if I was right, she wouldn't be the only one returning to their own self. It would also make the smile on Astrid's face just that little bit wider. I wasn't sure if I wanted to tell her what I thought. If I was wrong, it had the potential to hurt her more, but I needed someone on my side and without Hayden and Ari around to help, she was the only person I could think of that would be up for the adventure.

"Follow me," I said beckoning her with my hand. "We are going to get our boys back."

A boy recovered

Knowing what had happened was one thing, or at least, thinking I knew what had happened. Knowing where they were was another problem entirely. I had an inkling, but I didn't want to be sailing around forever looking for them. I grabbed Astrid's hand, and the pair of us headed downstairs. There only one person I needed to speak to, and I was pretty sure I knew where to find him. I opened the door to my father's conference room to find it packed to the gills with reporters. Only by standing on my tiptoes could I see my mother and father at the other end. As soon as the reporters saw that Astrid and I had entered the room, they swung around and began snapping photos of the two of us together. I guess finding out the queen was half mermaid wasn't enough for the press, they also had to expand on the switching brides too.

"Ladies and gentlemen," my father called out. "Please, can you let these fine ladies through?"

The group of reporters parted, leaving a small pathway for us to squeeze through.

"What is it, Erica?" asked my father as we neared the front.

"I was hoping to speak to Admiral Harrington-Blythe," I replied in a voice low enough so that the reporters wouldn't hear. "I thought he'd be in here with you."

My father shook his head and leaned in to me. "The old chap has taken a couple of personal days. I think the thought of bombing that underwater place affected him a bit. It's a good thing the water came back really. I'm not sure if he'd have been able to go through with it."

I raised my eyebrows. "You mean to tell me that the admiral hasn't been seen for three days?" The exact same three days that Hayden and Ari have been missing. Interesting!

"That's right." He turned to Astrid. "Oh, I love your new do. Very fetching. It almost looks like you've got the ocean on your head."

Astrid beamed. I grabbed her hand again and pulled her back through the crowd, ignoring the microphones thrust in our faces and the questions the reporters were throwing at us.

"Where are we going?" asked Astrid as I pulled her through the front door of the palace and ran down the long driveway.

"We are going to find out where Hayden and Ari are. I think Hayden's father might know. I just hope he isn't with them because if he is, I'm out of ideas of where to look."

There were no reporters by the front gates. They were all inside, but there were still plenty members of the public waiting there to get a photo of the palace or one of the members of the royal family. They were going to have a field day today because I planned to go through the gates.

The guards on the gates weren't too happy about me having them open the gates, but they had to do what I asked them. As an afterthought, I had one of them accompany us across the street. I'd been in Hayden's home many times over the years and had always been welcome, but now, when Hayden's father answered the door, he all but slammed it in my face.

"I'm looking for Hayden," I began. "I was wondering if he was home."

I knew full well he wasn't home, but I wanted the admiral to acknowledge the fact.

"I'm afraid he isn't," the admiral sniffed, trying to shut the door. The palace guard I'd asked to come with us wedged his foot in the door to stop it from closing entirely.

"Can you tell us where he is?" I asked again, this time trying to sound more confident. The truth was I'd always been a little scared of him, but I wasn't about to back down.

"No," he blustered. "I don't know where he is. I've not seen him for days, now if you wouldn't mind." He looked pointedly at the guard who looked to me for guidance. I shook my head.

"Admiral Harrington-Smyth," I started again, filling my voice with steel. "I think you do know where Hayden is. I think you just don't want to tell us. I'm not planning on leaving here until I get some answers!"

His face fell as he opened the door wider. "You'd better come in."

He shuffled to the living room where he called for his wife.

"Evaine, darling. Could you be a dear and get some tea for our guests?" Evaine Harrington-Blythe looked surprised to see us as she came into the room. "Erica, Astrid, how wonderful to see you both. If you are here to see Hayden, I'm afraid you are out of luck. He hasn't been home for days. Goodness only knows where he's taken himself off to."

"Yes, yes," said Henry impatiently. "Would you bring the tea for us and some of those wonderful cakes you made this morning."

She smiled and left the room. I had a feeling that wherever Hayden was, his mother knew nothing about it. His father on the other hand...

"You know where Hayden is?"

The Admiral shook his head. "Not exactly. He didn't tell me where he was going, but three days ago one of your father's naval ships was stolen. One of my senior men told me that they'd seen Hayden commandeering it."

"Commandeering?" asked Astrid.

"Stealing, hijacking, whatever you call it. He took the ship without my permission. That's why I've not been to work. I can't begin to think of a way to explain to your father, the king, why my son would steal one of his majesty's fleet."

"How did he manage to steal a ship?" I asked.

Henry raised his hands to the sides of his face and began to massage his temples. "He told the crew that he was there on my orders. It was one of the smaller vessels, but even so, sailing it on his own would be incredibly difficult. Almost impossible, I'd say."

"Do you think he might have someone with him?" I asked, thinking of Ari.

"It would make more sense for him to have another member of the crew on board, but all of the *Oceanis* crew...that's the name of the vessel, are accounted for. I've asked them to keep this quiet for now, but I knew it would get out eventually. I'll go and tell His Majesty this afternoon."

"Don't!" I replied quickly as he began to rise from his chair. He sat back down with a thump.

"My father is busy enough with the press, and I have no intention of telling him about this."

The admiral's face lit up, and he let out a long breath. "You won't?"

"No, but I do need to know where he is, so I can find him and bring him home. I'm also going to need a ship."

He looked at me in surprise. "I can't give you a ship. I've already managed to lose one, but I can lend you Hayden's boat. It's docked at the marina."

"Will you help me sail it?" Help was a loose term. I'd never sailed a ship before, and neither to my knowledge had Astrid. If he came with us, he'd be doing all the sailing.

"Of course," he replied, standing up. This time I let him.

We made a funny trio, running through the streets down to the dock. The palace guard was sent back to the palace to let my parents know what was going on. I'd be going out on the ocean again, but this time, with the sea witch being dead and with everything going on at the palace, I figured my mother would be ok with it.

Hayden's boat was really no more than a boat for day sailing. It did have a small bunk below deck, but I don't think Hayden had ever used it for anything other than storage. The sea was calm, although the clouds in the sky above made it dull. Not that it mattered. This was no sightseeing trip.

"Which way?" asked Henry as we cast off from the dock.

"I don't know, let's just get out to sea and take it from there."

I waited for either Henry or Astrid to tell me what a large place the ocean was, but neither did. Henry let the sails out, and Astrid sat near the front, peering out to sea. She was just as desperate to find Hayden as I was to find Ari. We sailed for hours with the wind at our backs. Hayden's boat might have been small, but it could move. Every time I saw a ship, my heart raced, but none of them were as large or majestic as the one Hayden stole from my father. As the light dimmed and the afternoon turned to evening, I had to make the decision to turn around. We were already going to be home way past dark. We'd survived the day on bottled water and a few provisions Hayden had left below deck, but there wasn't enough for another day.

I looked over at Astrid, feeling sad that I'd have to tell her that we were going to head home when her whole face lit up. She turned to me with a sparkle in her eyes and a smile on her face. She pointed outward toward the horizon. I followed the line of her finger and saw in the distance the outline of my father's missing ship.

"Henry!" I called back. "Head that way." He popped his head around the corner and peered out to where both Astrid and I were pointing. We had to hold on tightly while the boat lunged as it turned, almost spilling us over the side.

I fingered the ruby around my neck as we headed closer to the dark shape. If I was right, and I really hoped I was, it would save all of us and hopefully put things back to normal. The ship itself looked eerie, floating as it was in the purple dusk. There was no sign of life, which was to be expected as there were only two of them aboard, and they were more than likely inside. Even so, the sight of the massive ship looking empty, had me feeling a chill in my heart. Whatever it was that Hayden planned to do, I prayed that he'd not already gone ahead with it.

Henry docked alongside the great ship and tied Hayden's boat to it. There was no ladder for us to climb, but there were enough ropes for us to pull ourselves up onto the main deck.

"What now?" asked Astrid, looking as scared as I felt.

"Now we find them."

Finding them was not as difficult as I thought it would be, or at least, finding Ari wasn't. He was tied up in the captain's suite, a gag in his mouth.

His pupils dilated as he took the three of us in and he made a noise through the gag. I ran to him and untied the rag from around his face.

"Watch out!" he shouted, but it was too late. I turned to where he was looking to find Hayden standing in the corner with a gun pointing at us.

"Hayden!" Astrid, gushed, running toward him, but she stopped suddenly as the gun pointed at her.

"I wasn't expecting company," Hayden sneered. "Never mind, you can watch me push this guy overboard. It will be nice to have an audience."

"Pushing him overboard won't kill him," I pointed out, putting my body between Ari and the gun. "He can breathe underwater."

"No, you are right. A hole in the head before I send him to be fish food ought to do it, though, don't you think? I've been trying to muster up the courage to do this for three days, but now that you are here, I realize it's not courage I lack. I wanted someone to see me defeat him. I can't begin to tell you how glad I am that it's you."

I caught Henry's expression harden as he saw what his son was capable of.

"Hayden. What are you doing?"

Henry was rewarded with the gun moving from Astrid to him. None of us would be able to get close to him, not without gaining a hole in ourselves in the process.

"Hayden. This isn't you. I've figured it all out," I began. "I've come here to save you."

Hayden sneered "Save me? I think you've got it all wrong. It's your boyfriend you should be worried about. He's the one that's going to die, and maybe one of you if you try and get in my way." He spat the word *boyfriend* out.

"Hayden!" Astrid shouted out in shock, but he ignored her.

"It's not Hayden," I said. Astrid's eyes went wide as comprehension dawned on her face.

"Of course, it's me, you idiots. Who else would I be?"

"Let me rephrase then," I said, stepping slowly closer to him. "It is you, but you are under a spell. You've been behaving strangely for a while, and a few hours ago, I remembered when your personality change started. You were perfectly happy with Astrid before we went to visit the sea witch the first time. It was only afterward that you became angry. You claimed you were in love with me and were using Astrid, but that wasn't the case at all."

"Shut up. I asked Astrid to marry me. You have no idea what you are talking about." I could see him wavering as I spoke. His hand began to shake.

"But you think you love me, don't you? You only asked Astrid to get her off your back. You had no intention of marrying her. Isn't that right?"

I could see Astrid's resolve begin to crumble at this change of direction. I just needed her to be strong for a few more minutes.

"Untie Ari," I whispered to her as I walked past, getting closer to Hayden.

I heard her move behind me, but Hayden's eyes were right where I wanted them—on me.

"You are in love with me, aren't you? The girl who you pined after for years." I was so close to him now. If I wanted to, I could reach out and touch him. I could see his resolve begin to crack.

"Yes," he whispered. "I've always loved you. I never wanted Astrid. It was always you."

Behind me, I heard a scream, but it was not Astrid's voice I heard. It was Ari. I turned to see the look of agony on his face as Astrid untied his legs. The skin on his exposed ankles was almost raw, red and wet with patches of black.

My heart went into overdrive. The witch had lied to me. I don't even know why I was surprised, but it left me with a dilemma. The ruby had only enough magic to save one of them. I had to make the decision between Ari and Hayden, and I had to make it quickly.

"You don't love me, though. You love that bastard."

I turned back to Hayden to see him putting the gun up to his temple. With the speed of a cheetah, I grabbed the Havfrue ruby from around my neck and held it to Hayden's face.

Red light shone out from him as his piercing screams drowned out all other sounds. The gun dropped to the floor, and purple smoke began flowing from Hayden's ears, eyes, and pores. Seconds later, it was all over. Hayden fell to the floor in a heap. I kicked the gun away from him, although I knew he was no longer a threat. The spell was broken. Hayden was free. Astrid came running over and fell beside him, smothering him with a hug.

"What just happened?" asked Henry, a look of shock on his face. I probably should have warned him about my theory before we boarded the ship.

"He'll be fine," I said with a small smile. "Astrid, I'm sorry about all that. I just had to keep him talking while I got close enough to him. I think you'll find he'll be back to normal and completely in love with you just as he was before our first encounter with the witch."

Behind me, I heard a low moan. I turned back to Ari.

He no longer had ropes tying him to the chair, but he was, nevertheless, incapable of getting up from it. Blood seeped through his trousers, leaving sticky wet patches.

"Help me," I shouted at Henry, who still appeared dumbstruck with the turn of events. Between us, we managed to pull Ari's trousers from his legs and hurl him into the sea. In less than a minute he reappeared at the surface, his face no longer ashen, his tail appearing healthy behind him.

"Henry, can you get this ship turned around? We need to get everyone home."

He nodded and left me to steer the ship. Hopefully, Hayden's boat would be tied tightly enough, so it would float alongside.

I waved down at Ari, desperate to be in the water with him, but I had to see if Hayden was okay first.

"I'll be with you in a minute," I called down to him. He nodded and disappeared underwater.

Back in the captain's room, Astrid and Hayden were still crumpled on the floor, wrapped in each other's arms. I could hear one of them sobbing, although it was hard to tell which one.

"Henry is taking us home," I announced.

Hayden untangled himself and first pulled himself and then Astrid up. He walked over to me and hugged me tightly.

"Just so you know, this is just a hug of friendship," he grinned as he pulled away. Indeed, he did have tears in his eyes. They both did.

"I'm so sorry," he began, but I shushed him.

"It wasn't you. It was the spell."

"I do love you. You are my best friend, but..."

He turned and took Astrid's hand. She beamed.

"But you are in love with Astrid," I finished for him.

"I am." He turned to her. "I really am."

They kissed, absorbed only in each other. I was the gooseberry in this scenario. Quietly, I tiptoed for the door. There was somewhere I wanted to be more than with my two best friends anyway. I pulled off my shoes and ran to the deck. Without pausing, I climbed onto the railing and hurled myself into the dark water.

A warm hand took mine. We swam beside each other for hours, keeping the ship in our sights. As it pulled into the dock, Ari pulled me to the surface. The moon had come out lacing the ocean with a million sparkles. We'd not said a word to each other the whole trip back. We'd been too caught up with the freedom of the ocean, with each other, but now that we were back at the rocks, we had to talk.

"I don't know why I believed her," I said sadly, meaning the sea witch. "She told me that your legs would be better."

Ari took my face in his hands. It amazed me how warm he felt even though the water around us was freezing.

"She gave me my voice back," he said.

"It's not enough."

"It doesn't matter what she said or did. I'm just happy that you are alive. In my whole life, no one has ever done anything for me, and you gave your life for me."

As I gazed into his eyes, I knew I'd done the right thing. The outcome was not how I'd imagined it, but I'd do it all again in an instant to stop his pain.

"I wish I could have done more. I had one wish, and I used it on Hayden."

He traced a hand down my cheek, wetting his fingers with my tears.

"Erica, it was everything." As he leaned forward to kiss me, I wished I could believe his words, but the truth of the matter was, he was still hurting while on land, and nothing I had done could help him with that.

"The doctors said that they should be able to manage the pain with medication," he said lightly as he pulled away from me.

"The same medication that knocked you out? If you stay on land, you'll either be in pain or asleep"

My heart broke as I thought of the next words to come out of my mouth. I wanted to be selfish, to be greedy, and keep him with me always, but to do that would cause him more suffering.

"You have to go home."

He drew his lower lip between his teeth. "We are bonded. We can't be apart. I don't want to go home without you."

I could feel my heart tearing in two at his words. If he said much more, I'd tell him to forget the whole thing, but looking at him, I knew I couldn't. The sea witch could have made it possible for us to be together, just as she had for my parents, but the sea witch was dead along with her magic. Her final act had been to make our lives completely impossible. Destined to be together, but forced to live apart. We couldn't be on land because of the pain, I couldn't live under the sea because I'd have to be touching him to be able to breathe. We'd never be able to be apart for more than a few seconds at a time.

I kissed him then. A farewell kiss full of sadness and pain. Leaving him was going to kill me, but as with many things in life, I had no choice.

The walk back across the rocks was excruciating. I didn't look back as I walked. I couldn't bear to see that look on his face.

I saw the ship at the docks and three figures stepping off in the dark, two of which were holding hands. At least, something good had come of all this. Hayden and Astrid were now able to be together without anyone forcing them apart. My mother had been reunited with her father and would probably go and see her sisters soon, and the kingdoms of Havfrue and Trifork were now no longer mortal enemies. To top it all off, the witch who had terrorized the underwater world was dead. If I looked back at the events of the past few weeks, a lot of good had happened, and yet, my own life had derailed. I'd met the man I was supposed to spend the rest of my life with, and circumstances made it impossible for us to be together.

I plodded slowly to the palace, past the guards on duty and to my room where I fell on my bed. There were no tears, just a heart so heavy I thought it would sink me right into the mattress itself. I probably wouldn't have minded if it did.

I wondered if the pain I was feeling was something to do with the bonding. Ari had told me that the further we were apart, the more painful it would feel. I wasn't sure. I had a feeling I'd hurt like this even if we weren't bonded in a magical way. I'd never had a broken heart before, but this sure did feel like one.

With a sigh, I realized I'd feel this way always. The bonding had sounded so romantic when Ari told me about it, but now it was nothing more than a curse.

I closed my eyes and willed sleep to come to let me escape the pain I was feeling. The next morning, I woke late. My mother didn't come to wake me for my studies. Someone must have told her what happened, and she decided to let me sleep in. I dragged myself out of bed. There was no point wasting the day, no matter how awful I felt. My relationship with my mother had been mended somewhat, thanks to me bringing her father to her, but there was still a long way to go. I decided to go find her and ask her if she wanted to spend the day with me. We could sit outside in the gardens and just talk. It was way overdue.

I found her in the grand hall ordering workers to move boxes of stones and weird decorations. She had such a smile on her face. I don't think I'd ever seen her so happy.

For a brief second, I wondered if she had gone loopy again and was planning another wedding, albeit one with a strange theme.

"There you are sleepyhead," she smiled as she turned to me. She looked radiant. "What do you think?"

I gazed around the room at huge pieces of coral and boxes of sand that were being stacked up against the wall.

"Nice, what is it for?"

She came running over to me and slipped her arm in mine. In a quiet voice she spoke "My father came to visit me last night. He asked if my sisters could come visit. I'm planning a big family reunion. Half of Havfrue is coming. It's going to be huge."

Just then, I heard a noise. It sounded like a truck was parking outside.

"That will be the tank," she said, clapping her hands together. I followed her outside to where a massive tank was being placed in the gardens. It was huge and currently empty.

"The people from the Trifork Aquarium are setting it up. It needs pumps and filters for the fish, and it will take a week or so to fill with water, but everyone will feel at home."

I shook my head at the scale of what my mother could achieve when she put her mind to it. The woman never ceased to amaze me.

I felt an elbow digging into my side.

I looked at my mother, whose grin was now even larger if that were possible. "I think there is someone who'd like an invite. Tell him the party is on the fourteenth."

I looked to where my mother was pointing. Ari was sitting on the rocks, his tail dipping in the water.

Despite everything, despite the fact it was impossible for us to be together, I still ran to him.

"We are broken up," I sang, a smile on my face. My heart already felt a million times lighter. Maybe this bonding thing really did work.

"I know."

Without a goodbye, he dove neatly beneath the perfectly flat surface of the water, barely making a splash.

I waited for him to resurface, but the water remained almost glasslike, barely rippling.

My heart began to beat wildly. Was that it? He'd surely come to see me. Had he only come to say goodbye. He'd not even managed that.

I could barely catch my breath, now that he'd gone. There was no goodbye kiss, no farewell, nothing.

And then he breached the surface and held his hand out to me.

"You coming?"

I couldn't speak with the emotions tugging at me, pulling me in all directions.

"I can't come with you. You know that. We have to end it."

"Maybe," he said, "but not today."

With a grin, I pulled my dress over my head and dove into the ocean.

THE END

Coming soon... Blue Water (Little Mermaid Reverse Fairytale book 2)

If you enjoyed Dark Water, you might enjoy Beauty Sleep (Sleeping Beauty Reverse Fairytale book 1)

Beauty Sleep

"You drinking or am I gonna have to kick you out?"

I looked up into the eyes of the sweaty bartender-cum-club owner and put on my sweetest smile.

"Whiskey, straight up."

He leered slightly, showing yellowing teeth that looked like they'd never seen a toothbrush. His already narrow eyes turned into slits as if deciding whether to throw me out or not. Apparently not, as he turned back to the bar to fetch me my drink.

I'd not been in this particular cesspit of a bar before, but I'd been in plenty like it. Dark, filthy, the end of the line.

To my right was an old man slumped over his table snoring, his latest pint of beer only half drunk. No doubt the bartender would be moving onto him now that he was no longer a paying customer. It wasn't the man that held my interest, though. It was the group of men seated around a table in the corner playing poker.

Poker was the real reason I frequented dumps like this. Personally, I'd prefer to live it up in some of the nicer establishments in Eshen, but unfortunately for me, they either didn't allow gambling or in the case of the ones that did, I was already well known. I needed to be in a place where no one knew me to make money, not that it was money that had me trawling bars night after night. The money was just a bonus. No, the reason I chose illegal gambling as my chosen profession was much bigger than trying to get richer.

And so, I found myself having to travel further and further to find a good game. A game where I could win. Actually, that wasn't strictly true. I won most games. I needed a game where I could win and not get my face punched by some meathead sore loser which had happened enough for me to worry about it and usually happened at about the same time that I was recognized.

You see, I was the best damn poker player in a hundred square miles, but to win, I needed people to not know that. I needed them to think I was a helpless little girl, who didn't know a flush from a straight.

Being an actual little girl didn't hurt my ruse. Actually, I was twenty-two but so tiny I often passed as younger. I have that sweet and innocent look about me, thanks to my fae genes, which was the greatest irony. I smoked, I drank, and worst of all, I cheated. I cheated big time. Not that you'd ever guess with my wide green eyes and dark curls. Yeah, I was just the picture of innocence, which is why I generally kicked ass in a place like this.

And I really did kick ass. Sometimes, literally. I might be tiny, but as a member of the fae race, I've got powers that most others don't. It's not only poker that these meatheads lose along with their money; they also lose any dignity they have when a girl half their size kicks the crap out of them.

"Here!" The bartender slammed my drink down, sloshing half of it over the table. I knew better than to say anything. The game was heating up, and the last thing I wanted was to get thrown out before I even had a chance to play.

There were four of them playing and only four seats. Fine with me. Once one of them was out, I'd sidle up and take his spot...if, and only if, I decided it was worth it.

Sure, there was a great deal of money on the table, always a good sign. And three of the four looked like complete morons, thickset with meaty biceps and even meatier brains—ogres or, at least, part ogre. The fourth looked to be human although it was difficult to tell as he had his back to me.

His pile of coins was diminishing fast, much to the apparent joy of the others. I nursed my whiskey, or what was left of it, and watched the game play out. As soon as the human was out, I'd drink it down and take his place.

He held nothing of value in his hand, so he'd either have to bluff real good or lose everything. As I suspected, he lost the little bit of money he had. Knocking back the whiskey, I stood up. If the three meatheads were used to that level of play, I'd kick their asses.

The human didn't leave the table as I'd expected him to do. Instead, he leaned forward and whispered something to the men. All three of the bigger ones grinned broadly and then began to deal again. I called over the barman and ordered another whiskey.

Whatever the man had said, it had brought excitement to the table. The three ogres were practically salivating. This was getting interesting now.

The kid was either incredibly stupid, or he was playing my way. I grabbed the whiskey and headed to a table in the shadows, eager to see just how this was going to play out.

It was to be a one-round game. All three of the larger men went all in, so the center of the small table was filled with gold. It was so heavy, I was surprised that the crappy wooden table could hold it. Whatever the young man had put into the pot, I couldn't see, but it had to be something huge with all that gold on offer.

By the end of the game, I was on the edge of my seat, not even caring anymore if anyone saw me. If they were all in, I'd not be able to join. There'd be no point. I really should have left right there and then, but something stopped me. I genuinely wanted to know what was going to happen. . . The rest of the people in the bar watched along with me, as well as the bartender who'd temporarily forgotten he was there to serve drinks.

My knuckles were white, gripping the whiskey glass as the last of the three meatheads put down his cards. I couldn't see what he'd played, but judging by what the younger man had in his hand, the biggest meathead was going to win. Just as the younger man put his cards down, he reached up his sleeve and swapped his cards. It was so fast that I was sure I was the only one who noticed.

The guy was a sneaky cheat!

Ok, I had no room to talk, but he was so brazen. At least, I used magic to cheat. His cheating seemed so much worse somehow.

When the cards hit the table, the smirk on the big guy turned to a look of disbelief and then quickly to anger. He picked the young guy up by the scruff of the neck and punched him, sending him skidding backwards across the floor and landing right at my feet.

It was then that I saw his face for the first time. A face that I recognized instantly.

A face that anyone should recognize even covered in blood as it was. He was the Crown Prince of Eshen, His Royal Highness Prince Rory.

Now, what would the crown prince be doing in a place like this? I know I have no room to talk, but I had my reasons. I wondered what his were. Unlike me, he didn't need the money, so that couldn't be the reason. His parents were the king and queen for goodness sake. No one in the whole kingdom was richer than they were.

I should have run, especially when the three ogres threw their chairs to one side and started lumbering over towards me, but my curiosity got the best of me.

Whether the ogres knew who he was or not was beside the point. I knew guys like these. I'd met plenty in my time. There was no way Prince Rory was going to get out of here alive if they got their hands on him.

"Crap!" I cursed, under my breath. I'd hidden in the darkest corner of the room precisely because I didn't want to be seen and I didn't want any trouble. It was too late for that now. Trouble headed towards me in the form of three butt-ugly ogres. I downed my whiskey—there was no way I was going to leave it—and stood up to face the three men.

When they saw me, they laughed, all three of them gurning as their lips curled up at the edges, twisting their features hideously.

With my two arms in front of me, hands clenched into fists, I snarled at them. The noise sounded like a puppy mewling. I am the first to admit that I hardly cut an imposing figure. Still, you have to work with what you've got. "I don't want to have to fight you guys, but if you touch him again, I'll be forced to kick your butts."

They stopped in surprise. Not one of them was expecting someone of my size to stand up to them. Then they laughed again, this, a little too hard. It really hurt my feelings. The first didn't know what was coming as I landed a punch right on his jaw, sending him backwards into the poker table and scattering the gold coins onto the floor. . .

Before meathead two had a chance to respond, I kicked him squarely between the legs, dropping him to the floor.

The biggest of the lot charged towards me, sending me backwards into the wall with his bulky mass.

He pulled back his fist. Most men wouldn't hit a woman, especially a woman so small, but he had no such qualms. I ducked to the right just in time to feel his fist go right through the plaster on the wall sending dust and rubble all over my jacket.

"I just bought this!" I hissed, dusting the shoulder where bits of gray wall now decorated it.

Being held up as I was, jammed between him and the wall, I didn't have a lot of options for fighting back. . . I pulled back my elbow right to the wall and with as much force as I could muster, punched him in the face. He didn't even blink.

Dribble escaped the corner of his mouth as his fetid breath hit my nose. We were eye to eye now although my feet were a good two feet from the ground, and judging by the leer he was giving me, punching me was getting further and further from his mind as he worked out what else he could do to me.

"Over my dead body!" I screamed, trying to push the brute away, but it was no use. He was so much stronger than I, even with fae blood running through my veins.

Being this close to him, I could see that my first impression was true. He was definitely at least part ogre which meant he had no empathy or guilt at all. He'd crush me without shedding a tear.

There was only one course of action left to me, and it was the one thing I'd hoped to avoid. Still, it was better than being killed by this thug or worse.

My wings were safely hidden, curled up in the back of my jacket and currently crushed against the wall, but I didn't need them to use magic. Instead, I closed my eyes and concentrated. Five seconds later, I'd built up the energy I needed to blast him. With a flash of light, the meathead flew through the air, leaving an ogre-sized hole in the plaster at the other side of the bar.

I looked on the floor for the prince. He'd disappeared. When I looked up, I saw that the giant pile of gold had also gone.

Unfortunately, the three ogres were still there and judging by the looks of them, they were really pissed off. They picked themselves up and headed towards me. My magic was depleted, and there was no way I'd be able to fight them off a second time. Pulling my jacket off, I spread my wings and flew as quickly as I could out of the bar and escaped into the night.

When I felt I'd put enough distance between me and the bar, I floated back down to the ground in a dark street.

The dead-end street was deserted with only a lone flickering streetlamp lighting it. Wildfell was one of Eshen's seedier cities, and I was in a particularly rough part. Very few people ventured out at this time of night around here which is why I was surprised to see someone hiding in the shadows not ten feet away from me. He was nothing more than a shadow. Most people would have walked right past him and not even noticed he was there, but my fae senses noticed him immediately. He was a man, a tall man, and from the way he was hunched over, I could see he was injured.

Not my problem

I wandered down the road in his direction, wondering if it was the prince. As I got close, I saw it was, his bloodied and battered face, still dripping onto the bag of loot. He was so caught up in counting his new found gold that he didn't notice me walk right up to him. Was this guy for real? He was happy to steal from ogres but too stupid to get far enough away before counting the treasure.

"You're a brave man to steal money from ogres," I commented, bringing a cigarette from a crumpled box in my pocket and lighting it.

The prince quickly glanced my way and took off again, spilling gold coins as he ran.

Good. I figured the guy owed me anyway. If I'd not have been in the bar, helping him out, he'd probably not have made it out alive.

I followed his trail of coins, stopping to pick up each one in the dim light until I got to the end of the street.

The prince had run himself into a dead-end and was now crouching in a corner trying not to be seen.

"So much for being brave, huh?" I shouted out to him. "Just stupid maybe."

Ok, it was practically treason calling a member of royalty stupid, but I figured he deserved it. Besides, what exactly could he do? If he had me arrested, he'd have to explain where he was, and I figured he wouldn't want to do that.

"I'll give you half my money if you let me pass," he shouted out.

Interesting! He'd won a fair wad of cash, more than I had expected to win when I first walked into the bar. I suspected his offer had less to do with the fact he had seen me beat up the ogres and more to do with me keeping my mouth shut. I took a drag on my cigarette and inhaled deeply.

"You've got a deal, Your Highness."

I emphasized the Your Highness bit. If I could get even more money out of him, it was worth a try.

He slowly ambled over to me, a look of wariness in his eyes.

"Thanks for helping me out back there," he said, handing me a small bag he'd filled with coins. I could tell by the weight it wasn't half of his winnings.

"No problem," I replied, dropping the cigarette to the floor and stamping it out with my booted toe.

Up close, he was good-looking. I'd only ever seen him smartly dressed with perfect hair on TV, but now that he was in front of me and covered in blood, he'd taken on a dangerous quality. It suited him, made him more real somehow. His usual clean-shaven face had a layer of stubble covering his chiseled chin, and his light blue eyes regarded me warily. I could tell he didn't do this kind of thing often. . .

I was just about to ask him for more money, ok, extort more money from him, when I heard voices behind me. I turned to find the three ogres heading quickly towards us. A ping sound followed closely by a bang told me they'd brought guns with them.

Without thinking, I put my arms around the prince and took off into the sky.

It was only when I landed three miles away by my home that I realized I'd been shot.

Buy Beauty Sleep on Amazon now

34676373R00202

Printed in Great Britain
by Amazon